SPLIT THE SKY

SPLIT THE SKY

MARIE ARNOLD

LITTLE, BROWN AND COMPANY

New York Boston

This book is a work of fiction. Names, characters, places, and incidents are the product of the author's imagination or are used fictitiously. Any resemblance to actual events, locales, or persons, living or dead, is coincidental.

Copyright © 2025 by Marie Arnold

Cover art copyright © 2025 by Zharia Shinn
Cover copyright © 2025 by Hachette Book Group, Inc.
Interior design by Amanda Kain.

Hachette Book Group supports the right to free expression and the value of copyright. The purpose of copyright is to encourage writers and artists to produce the creative works that enrich our culture.

The scanning, uploading, and distribution of this book without permission is a theft of the author's intellectual property. If you would like permission to use material from the book (other than for review purposes), please contact permissions@hbgusa.com. Thank you for your support of the author's rights.

Little, Brown and Company
Hachette Book Group
1290 Avenue of the Americas, New York, NY 10104
Visit us at LBYR.com

First Edition: September 2025

Little, Brown and Company is a division of Hachette Book Group, Inc. The Little, Brown name and logo are registered trademarks of Hachette Book Group, Inc.

The publisher is not responsible for websites (or their content) that are not owned by the publisher.

Little, Brown and Company books may be purchased in bulk for business, educational, or promotional use. For information, please contact your local bookseller or the Hachette Book Group Special Markets Department at special.markets@hbgusa.com.

Library of Congress Cataloging-in-Publication Data
Names: Arnold, Marie, author.
Title: Split the sky / Marie Arnold.
Description: First edition. | New York : Little, Brown and Company, 2025. | Audience: Ages 12 & up. | Summary: "In a town with growing racial tension, a young Black girl must use her powers of foresight to save an unarmed teen from being killed." —Provided by publisher.
Identifiers: LCCN 2024037307 | ISBN 9780316582872 (hardcover) | ISBN 9780316582933 (ebook)
Subjects: CYAC: Race relations—Fiction. | Ability—Fiction. | Precognition—Fiction. | African Americans—Fiction. | LCGFT: Novels.
Classification: LCC PZ7.1.A7632 Sp 2025 | DDC [Fic]—dc23
LC record available at https://lccn.loc.gov/2024037307

ISBNs: 978-0-316-58287-2 (hardcover), 978-0-316-58293-3 (ebook)

Printed in Indiana, USA

LSC-C

Printing 1, 2025

*Dedicated to my sister, Cindy, and my parents:
I could not have done this without all of you.
This one is for the culture.*

*Also thank you to Jeff Potts and Oskar Karst,
for answering all my classical music questions,
and to Ian, Alex, and Rocky Moersen, my awesome
neighbors who sent them my way (and who loan me
their tools all the time).*

The very serious function of racism is distraction. It keeps you from doing your work. It keeps you explaining, over and over again, your reason for being.

—Toni Morrison

Struggle is a never-ending process. Freedom is never really won, you earn it and win it in every generation.

—Coretta Scott King

ONE

I DON'T THINK I'M GOOD AT BEING A BLACK GIRL. My voice doesn't harness the power of raging rivers or split the sky in half, like all the Black poets promised it would. I don't leave others amazed, mystified, or utterly beguiled. That's what's supposed to happen when you're magic. The thing is, not all Black girls want to be magic; some of us just want to *be*. But I'm not sure that's allowed here in Davey, Texas.

The north side of Davey—with very few exceptions—is all white. The south side, where we live, is the Black part. Recently, a group called People of Color for Progress

(PCP), made up of mostly Black residents, has been trying to change that.

There's always been an uneasy alliance between the white folks in the north and the Black folks on the south side, and thanks in part to PCP, things have ramped up.

My dad's voice snaps me out of my thoughts and back into my bedroom, where I'm holding the flyer that's made me so pensive.

"Lala Russell, are you ready?" he shouts up the stairs. Everyone calls me Lala, but my real name is Laveau. It was my grandma Sadie's idea. She insisted that I be named after Marie Laveau, the voodoo queen of New Orleans. She told my parents that she sensed a mystical presence when she first laid eyes on me. I don't know if they believed her or not. But they gave in.

"I'm almost ready!" I shout back. It's not true. I'm nowhere near ready. Tonight, we're having dinner with the woman Dad's been dating for the past two months. It's my and my twin brother's first time meeting her, and Dad's a little nervous. He's been fluffing pillows that don't need to be fluffed, sweeping parts of the house that were already clean, and rearranging the knickknacks he already arranged moments before.

I put the flyer on my desk and go over to my closet. I need to wear something nicer than the jeans and T-shirt I wore to school this morning. Before I can pick something out, the flyer draws my attention again. It could be the neon-green paper it's printed on, or the big, bold font. It could also be their new logo—a black fist that's pumping in the air with a treble clef cut out in the center. But for whatever reason, it pulls my attention. Someone slid it into my locker at school today. I go back to my desk, pick up the flyer, and read it for a third time.

**JOIN BLACK ALLIANCE CLUB!
HELP US SEND
A MESSAGE:
WE DON'T WANT
CONFEDERATE FLAGS AROUND.
TAKE IT DOWN!
TAKE IT DOWN!
TAKE IT DOWN!**

I agree with Black Alliance; a Confederate flag does not belong in Lawrence Ross Academy of Music. It's a prestigious school that prides itself on music excellence.

But like everything in Davey, our school is stuck in the past. If we were to get the flag situation fixed, another race-related issue would soon pop up. There's always some race-based problem to rage, fight, and protest against.

Who wants to spend two afternoons a week trying to combat race issues? Not me. So yeah, I guess I really am doing a bad job at being a good Black girl.

Here's the thing: a year after my mom passed away, my dad took us to her favorite place, Port Aransas beach. I had just started locing my hair and I made the unwise decision to roll around and get sand all through it. Aunt J washed and shampooed my hair thoroughly when I got home that night. And yet, days later, I found tiny grains of sand still caught in my locs. No matter what I did, I could never get all of it out.

That's racism in a nutshell. I can't pick it out, wash it out, or comb it out. No matter what I do, it's always going to be there. The racism in this town is like those stubborn grains of sand, only multiplied. Somehow, it's embedded under my nails, in the crease of my elbow, in the space between my lashes, and in my teeth. That's why I can't wait to get out of here.

I have a limited amount of time to make my mark in the world, and I don't want to spend it trying to fix small-town racism. Take, for example, my favorite cellist, Jacqueline Mary du Pré. When she was twenty, she recorded composer Edward Elgar's cello concerto with the London Symphony Orchestra. Her playing was aggressive and yet measured and graceful. It would go on to be considered one of the best performances in classical music history. Watching that concert was like the first time hearing Ella Fitzgerald scat, Kendrick Lamar spit, or Jazmine Sullivan riff: observing a thing of beauty.

But eight years later, Jacqueline was diagnosed with multiple sclerosis and forced to stop playing. I cry thinking of all the music she never got to make. In my head, Jacqueline and I were the same: We loved music so much, we made it our breath.

How much will I have accomplished before my music stops? Will I have had enough time to influence the classical music world? I've made a list of the ten great concert halls around the globe that I want to play in someday. What if I only get halfway down the list? I know my destiny is to play awe-inspiring music in breathtaking venues.

I know not every soon-to-be fifteen-year-old thinks so deeply about the finiteness of time, but I do. It could be because my mom died when I was only ten. It might be because timing is a key element in music. Or maybe it's because it seems like every other month, someone who looks like me ends up on a poster with the phrase SAY HER NAME.

No matter what the reason, I get that time is fleeting. I don't want to waste it joining Black Alliance or any other club that focuses on grains of sand I will never be totally free of. Instead, I choose to focus on playing my cello. Music never asks me to defend my right to exist or apologize for it.

I'm pretty sure I know who left this flyer for me: the founder of Black Alliance, Zora Carter. You know the moment a match is struck and a burst of flame roars to life? Zora is that moment and that burst of flame.

Everything about her is dynamic—from her freckled cinnamon complexion to her carefree hippie aesthetic. Her spiky, free-form locs are improvisational jazz; they abide by no rules. She plays the trumpet with the skill of a budding Louis Armstrong and the swagger of Miles Davis.

I'd like to be her for a day, or maybe two. She's never had a thought that she didn't voice, never met a Black cause that she didn't want to champion. Her refusal to do anything conventional, even small things like wearing matching socks, makes her a walking revolution. That said, I really wish she'd stop putting flyers in my locker and hitting me up on every social media there is, asking me to join.

I'm always nice when I reject her invites because I get why the club is important. The thing is, I don't need the added pressure of trying to right all the race-related wrongs that exist. It's hard enough just trying to walk between two worlds.

In school, I'm one of six Black kids in a specialized

music program; I have hair my classmates don't understand and a complexion that garners assumptions. In my neighborhood, the kids think I'm uppity and accuse me of speaking a different color than everybody else. I don't fit comfortably in either world.

I guess you could say it's my fault. I'm the one who fell in love with classical music. Looking back, if I'd known that playing the cello would make me an outcast on my street, I'd have never picked up the instrument. The way my dad tells it, the cello didn't give me a choice. According to him, I was three years old when I saw a live concert featuring acclaimed cellist Yo-Yo Ma on TV. I was in a trance for the duration of the piece. It was Bach: Cello Suite No. 1. And after that day, I was hooked.

All my cellos have been named Grace. When Grace and I first met, it wasn't instant love. Sometimes, I'd get frustrated and yell at her. I even kicked her once. After that particularly difficult lesson, my dad assumed I was done with cello. And yet, the next day, I was at it again. I dabble with a few other instruments: viola, violin, and a little piano. However, my heart will always belong to the cello.

Over the years, I've won countless competitions and received an armful of awards. I can't lie, I was kind of feeling myself. And then came the Monroe Competition. That day really messed me up for a while.

I push that memory away and focus on what I know will be the trajectory of my life once I'm done with high school in two years. I'll go to the most esteemed music conservatory on the East Coast—the Juilliard School—and from there, it's only a matter of time before I reach my ultimate goal: first chair in the New York Philharmonic. I don't care how many mountains I have to move, or stars I need to realign—one day, I, Lala Russell, will make it happen. I will get out of this stagnant town and live a totally different life in New York.

My first major step was getting into the Ross Academy. The school is ridiculously expensive and only gives out partial scholarships. My dad had to find a way to come up with the other half of my tuition. He took on another job and a loan from the bank. When I look into my dad's eyes, I see my dreams reflected. Sometimes that drives me to work even harder; other times, it fills me with panic to think I might fall short of what we both expect from me.

"Lala, you don't sound ready!" Dad scolds.

"How does someone 'sound' ready?" I ask myself out loud. I throw the flyer in the trash. I'm tempted to go down to the basement and play Grace. The only problem is, I've just come back from school, where I had a three-hour practice session. I learned early on that my drive and my body aren't always on the same page. So, in order to avoid tendinitis in my pinky, shoulder pain, back pain, and myriad other things, I have to pace myself.

I also know if my dad hears anything other than the sound of my getting ready, he's gonna lose it. So instead I focus on getting dressed.

I change into black slacks and a dressy blouse. I look myself over in the floor-length mirror. It's eerie sometimes how much I look like my mom. I have her big brown eyes, small frame, and mahogany complexion. After she died, I wanted to pay tribute to her by getting locs just like her. Fortunately, I'm related to the best hairstylist in the state, my aunt J. She hooked me up. And now I look even more like she did when she was my age. That's why I know I'm pretty—I look like my mom, and she was beautiful.

"Lala, don't make me call you again!"

Damn. I better get going.

Once I enter the hallway, the scent of rosemary bread and roasted chicken hits my nostrils and makes my mouth water. I head toward the kitchen to see what I can pilfer before dinner.

"Don't you do it!" my brother, Arlo, warns from the doorway of the dining room.

Although we're twins, we look nothing alike. Arlo favors my dad, with his dark complexion and impressive height. He doesn't have any muscles, but it's not from a lack of trying. He has what he calls a "swimmer's build." That's just a fancy way of saying he's on the thinner side.

Arlo is the chef in the family. When Aunt J taught him, she had no idea how well he'd take to cooking. In a few years, it became his thing. He wants to go to culinary school on the East Coast and open his own restaurant someday.

Sometimes, he gets on my last good nerve. And yet, no matter how much we bicker, I'll never deny his talent for cooking. That boy can burn! Or as Aunt J likes to say, "That boy put his foot in that dinner!"

"Arlo, I'm just gonna taste a small—"

"The hell you will," he says, blocking my path to the kitchen. He hates when people pick at his food. He insists it ruins the presentation. It's all I can do not to give him the biggest side-eye in history.

"C'mon, Arlo, please—"

"No!" he says.

"Fine!" I reply. He signals for me to join him in the dining room. We stand aside and watch Dad as he mulls over what the correct distance should be between the salad fork and the dinner fork. Dad has gone on a few dates in the last year. He's even had one or two of them over for dinner. So why is he so on edge and acting like he's never done this before?

Arlo and I think it might have something to do with her being white. Her name is Candace. According to the rundown Dad gave us, she recently moved here from Atlanta. She bought an art gallery on the north side. She loves jogging and has an extensive collection of blues albums.

I'm not tripping about Candace being white. My dad vets people very carefully. So I'm relatively sure his new girlfriend isn't a member of or sympathetic to the KKK. Which is not always a given here in Davey, former home to Faith & Honor, an offshoot of the Klan.

When Dad told us about Candace, he assured us that they were careful about where they went and how late they stayed out. That's not something that he would have had to mention last year; things are different now.

"How long has he been messing with the tableware?" I ask Arlo in a whisper.

Arlo shrugs and says, "About ten minutes. Why is he acting like this, for real?"

I remind Arlo about all the stories Dad has told us about growing up in Chicago. And how his grandmother would look him over to make sure he was dressed proper before he left the house. She'd say, "Don't you go out there lookin' crazy in front of all those white folks." I suggest maybe that's why he's overdoing it.

"Maybe..." Arlo replies skeptically.

Dad takes a last look at the table setting and gives it a nod of approval. He checks his watch and goes to the living room. We follow him out of sheer curiosity. We've never seen our dad so angst-ridden.

"This is a good idea. I've been alone for a while now... It's not wrong to want a personal life. Why should this be a big deal? It's not..." Dad says, answering his own question.

Arlo and I exchange a look. Dad is doing something he rarely does—explain his actions to us.

"You two are really gonna like her. You don't *have* to like her, I mean. Although I'm sure you will. I think. If you two aren't feeling her, it's fine. There's no pressure. I wanted you both to get to know her. Maybe it's too soon. Or maybe it's just the right time. This was a good idea," he says, filled with uncertainty. He goes over to the corner of the living room and checks himself out in the mirror hanging above the bar cart.

My parents were only seventeen when they had us. So as far as adults go, Dad's still pretty young. And according to many Black women in the neighborhood, he's very handsome. If anything, it's *them* he's gonna need to explain himself to.

"Small Fry, you need to engage," he says to me.

"But—"

"I know how you feel about small talk, Lala. Tonight, however, I need you to put that aside," he says.

I groan and drop my head like a five-year-old. I can't help it. I'm not good at chitchat.

"I'm waiting. Promise to talk and be social," he warns. I nod slowly and silently curse any and all dating apps.

He turns to my brother. "Arlo, here's what I need from you—" Dad begins.

Arlo cuts him off. "I know, I promise to engage," he says slyly.

"No! That's okay," Dad says quickly.

I swallow my laugh, knowing very well what he means. Arlo has a black belt in sarcasm.

"I think for you, less is more," Dad says tactfully.

I turn to my brother. "He means he wants you to shut up—like the rest of us."

"You see how she starts?" he says to Dad.

"Me?" I reply innocently. We start bickering back and forth in the time-honored tradition of siblings everywhere. My dad claps his hands triple time. We fall silent.

"I told Candace that I wanted her to meet my family. Don't make me regret this."

I'm not sure if it's a twin thing, but I can always tell when my brother is about to start some mess.

Arlo tilts his head up slightly and taps his index finger

to his chin, as if he's thinking really hard. "It seems odd to invite Candace over on a random weeknight. It's Monday. Shouldn't this be, like, a weekend thing? That way, Aunt J could join us," he says, feigning innocence.

I know exactly where he's going with this, and so does Dad. Before she opened her beauty shop, Aunt J used to temp for various businesses. She was always fine in the beginning, but eventually she'd get fired because she'd mentally check out. It made sense because the only things that held her interest long term were doing hair, cooking, and Nigerian soap operas.

Once Aunt J was fired, the same routine would play out between her and Dad: She'd come home and rant to him, "Earl, do you know them white folks had the nerve to fire me?"

My dad would then reply to his little sister, "Janice, last month you were fired for the same thing by Black people. Why weren't you upset then?"

She'd go on a diatribe about how Black people fired her first thing in the morning. Straight up. No games. On the other hand, white people fired her at the end of a shift— after a whole day of smiling in her face. She'd shake her head and conclude, "Nope, you can't trust them folks, no way." The two of them would argue and go at it. It always ended up with Aunt J calling him Earl Jr. just to annoy him. Due to their strained relationship, Dad never liked that he was named after his father. Grandpa Earl was a jazz musician and he'd be gone for long stretches of time. Dad always considered him mostly an absentee father.

Mondays are Aunt J's late day, and she won't be home until after dinner. So I totally get why Dad picked tonight of all nights to invite Candace over. There's no telling what would fly out of Aunt J's mouth if she were here.

Arlo turns toward me. "Lala, isn't it funny that out of all the days to invite a date over, Dad chooses the very night Aunt J won't be home?"

I know I shouldn't join in, but it's too hard to resist. "I'm sure that's just a coincidence. Maybe we can get her to close the shop early?" I suggest.

"Your aunt and Candace will meet each other—another time," Dad asserts.

We both smirk. Dad doesn't share our amusement. I try to let him off the hook. "Dad, it's fine that you're seeing a white lady," I assure him.

Arlo raises his hand. "I'm not judging either, Dad."

Relieved, Dad smiles. "Thank you, Arlo."

My brother is not done.

"Although you seeing a woman outside our race does send mixed signals to your children. I mean, what are we to think?" Arlo asks.

I shrug. "I don't think anything—well, except that my dad hates Black women."

Dad's face crumbles. He'd made it a point to tell us that dating outside of his race didn't mean he was rejecting Black women. We could have been good kids and reassured him that we were fine with whomever he decided to date. Instead, we use his fear against him because, well, it's just much more fun.

We start laughing and fist-bump.

"Nice one, Arlo."

"Team effort, sis."

Dad takes a big breath and exhales deeply, relieved that we were only joking.

"Dad, are you and Candace serious?" Arlo asks.

We study Dad's reaction. He gets this faraway look on his face, like he's recalling their previous encounters. And then he smiles like Homer Simpson in proximity of a donut.

My stomach does a somersault worthy of Simone Biles. I spit out the question, even though I'm pretty sure I'm not ready to hear the answer. "Are you in love with her?"

TWO

I NEVER THOUGHT I'D HEAR MYSELF ASKING DAD something like that. I know it's crazy, but I thought he'd never love anyone other than Mom.

"Dad, are you—*in love?*" I ask again.

He shoves his hands deep inside his pockets and shrugs his shoulders. "It's early, but..." The words he isn't saying are loud and heavy.

"I'm gonna go check on dinner," Arlo says, escaping to the kitchen before we can say anything.

"He's upset," Dad says quietly.

I shrug. "You know Arlo—he just has to be dramatic. He'll be fine."

He sits on the edge of the sofa and hangs his head.

"Dad, I vow to say words. Lots and lots of words."

He looks up and smiles. "Thanks."

"I'm gonna help Arlo with the food."

I enter the kitchen, where the chef is attending to the chicken in the oven. Outside the window, our next-door neighbors—an elderly couple, Mr. and Mrs. Brown—paint over the red graffiti spray-painted on their porch. It happened last night. They went to bed and woke up to find someone had sprayed the N-word on their property. Dad offered to help, but they said they had it handled. The week before, two blocks over, Ms. Hardy's door was also spray-painted.

This kind of stuff started to happen more often once PCP bought an apartment building in the heart of North Davey called Millwood Manor. They intend to offer housing at an affordable price, the goal being to diversify North Davey. The Manor is set to open a week from tomorrow. In fact, to drive home the point that they want things to change, PCP is having their grand opening in the evening—a time most Black folks know to avoid the north side.

Many of the north side residents see this as "the Blacks taking over." And so they come to the south side and vandalize our homes to show their displeasure. There have been protests from various groups in front of the building every day for months.

The protesters were met by a group of counterprotesters who are determined to make sure the Manor opens and welcomes as many people of color as possible. The closer we get to the grand opening, the more intense the battle seems to get between the two groups.

Despite that, the list of Black families who are set to move in is long. It's so long, there's a waiting list. The north side has a better school system, and the city maintains the parks and public buildings there routinely, unlike here on the south side. Lastly, the city spends more money on ensuring public safety on the north side.

Not all the Black residents agree with what's happening, though. Some of them blame PCP for stirring up trouble. They feel that while things in Davey aren't perfect, at least they have been peaceful.

The spray-painting incident at Ms. Hardy's was reported to the cops. A handful of people, including my dad, helped her clean up. Dad made us come along. While the adults closer to Dad's age vented and cursed at what happened, older residents seemed more put out than pissed off. Someone in the crowd I didn't recognize stood up and raged, "I'm new here; someone explain what's happening. When the hell did we go back to 1954?"

Ms. Hardy scoffed and said, "In America, it's always 1954 somewhere."

The crazy thing was no one in the room could find a way to counter that argument. I guess they've all been to places that are somehow locked in time.

Not everyone on the north side is part of a hate group, but it's not uncommon to see people there sporting jewelry, clothing, and tattoos that depict symbols proclaiming "white power."

And no one here on the south side would be shocked if any of these symbols were found on members of our county sheriff's department. The older Black residents have always called Davey a "best get town," as in, "You best get your Black behind back to the south side before dark." That's why we mostly stay on the south side. To me, living in a sundown town is like living in the shadow of an active volcano—I know it'll erupt, but I hope it won't be today.

The scent of fresh apple tarts fills my nose and rips me away from the window. Arlo adjusts the tarts on the baking sheet and then closes the oven door. While he's turned away from me, I smack him upside his head.

"Hey! What the hell, Lala?"

I try to whisper so we won't be overheard. "What's wrong with you? Didn't we say that since you and I would be headed for college in only two years, Dad would need someone?" I remind him.

"Yeah," he grumbles as he walks toward the window. The Browns have gone inside. There's no one else out there except a few kids playing football.

"What's the problem?" I demand. "You mad 'cause she white?"

He sucks his teeth loudly. "It's not that," he swears as he leans against the window. "La, did you see Dad's face just now? He was rocking the goofiest grin when he talked about her. He's not tripping because his new girl is white; he's tripping because he's falling in love with her! Doesn't that bother you?"

"No," I lie.

He gives me the side-eye, another thing he's mastered.

"Okay, maybe it did—a little. So?"

His jaw drops. "So that's Mom's smile. It belongs to her. Now he's handing it out to some chick we never met before?" He shakes his head.

"You're acting like you're five, not fourteen—about to be fifteen. Dad told you he was bringing her for dinner," I point out.

"Yeah, but he didn't tell me he invited his boyish charm to dine with us, too!" Arlo says through gritted teeth.

Dad's reaction comes back to me. "He did look a little... gaga. Didn't he?"

"See? This isn't just a 'meet my date' dinner. What if he's trying to ready us for 'meet your new mom'?"

Gray spirals flash.

Leather rocket.

Gust of wind.

Dance of glass.

"Arlo, move away from the window."

"Thanks," he says. He steps away from the window and comes to the other side of the kitchen.

"You're doing too much. It's dinner, not a proposal," I remind him.

He looks pensive and dejected. "Yeah, maybe."

We both stay silent for a moment.

"La... what do you remember most about her?"

I tell Arlo the first thing that comes to mind when I think of our mom: the smell of jasmine. On school nights, she used to do my hair, and I could smell the jasmine-scented essential oil she dabbed on her wrists. Whenever I would cry about something or have a bad day, she'd hug me and I'd inhale that scent. The smell calmed me down even before Mom's pep talk. Although she passed away, to this day, when I smell jasmine, a part of me still expects her to be somewhere nearby. That's usually followed by a dull ache in my chest when I remember that she's gone.

"When I think of Mom, I see her in the kitchen mixing batter and gathering all the ingredients for whatever she was baking. She'd turn, see me in the doorway, and give me this radiant smile..." he says, far away.

"I was always trying to sneak a taste of her food," I admit.

"Yeah, and *always* before the food was ready," he replies, annoyed.

"I was on the job. I was Mom's professional taster," I add proudly.

I do remember our mom in this very room, cooking up a storm of delicious meals. She loved making desserts. Arlo and I used to fight over who would get to lick the spoon and mixing bowl.

He grows quiet. Anytime he brings up Mom, it's usually followed by silence. My dad is the same way. That's why he rarely talks about her or their lives together. It's been five years, but her death still hurts like it happened yesterday.

Arlo needs a distraction. I look at all the food he has laid out for dinner. "All right. Take me through the menu. Tell me what you did to make everything smell so good."

He grins and eagerly starts boasting.

Five minutes later, we're almost through Arlo's detailed play-by-play of the menu when a football flies though the kitchen window, shattering the glass. The wind blows into the room as glass rains down.

Like I said, not all Black girls want to be magic.

But some of us don't have a choice. The fact is, like it or not, sometimes I can see the future.

I can't see every single thing that's about to happen before it does. I don't know what numbers will be called in next week's lotto; I've no idea who'll win the Super Bowl or when Rihanna's gonna grace us with new music. I don't control what I see or when I see it. It's kind of like yawning. You don't know when it's going to happen; it just does. It's a brief and involuntary occurrence that I live with.

"What's going on in there?" Dad shouts.

"Football from next door came through the window—we're fine. Cleaning up the glass now!" I shout back.

"I'll get the broom," Arlo says.

"It's okay. I got it. You start bringing the food out to the table and try to look happy, okay? Don't stress Dad out."

"Fine. But I'm not calling that lady Mom," Arlo warns.

He starts taking the dishes to the dining table one by one. I get the broom and begin sweeping the kitchen floor.

✦ 24 ✦

It reminds me of the first time I got a premonition. There was broken glass that day, too.

Arlo and I were five years old, and we went to New Orleans to stay with Grandma Sadie for the summer. There was a pitcher of sweet tea on the table. I picked up a mop and a rag and stood in the middle of the kitchen, waiting.

Grandma said, "What you doing with that? I just cleaned up the floor this morning, little girl." I shrugged because I didn't know how to explain to her that I had seen the fate of the pitcher. Then, about five minutes later, Arlo and some of his friends were running around and accidentally bumped the table. It knocked the glass pitcher over and it shattered on the floor.

Grandma Sadie looked at me from across the kitchen, her expression a mix of pride and worry. When we were done helping her clean, she picked up her basket of pea pods and told me to follow her out to the backyard. We sat on the steps, side by side, and began shelling the peas. She was quiet for a moment before she spoke.

"You seen the pitcher fall before it actually fell, Lala?"

I nodded. I wasn't sure why, but I thought maybe I was in trouble. I thought I had done something to make the pitcher *want* to fall over.

I guess she could see the worry on my face, because

she leaned in and whispered, "It's all right, child. You ain't done nothing wrong."

"I saw what was going to happen!" I protested.

"Yes, I know. I see things, too," she whispered.

"Really? Is something wrong with us?" I asked.

"Wrong? Hush, little girl. There's nothing wrong with you or me. Lala, what you experienced is what we in our family call Flashing. It's the ability to see a small fraction of what has yet to happen."

"Can anyone see it? Can my mom and dad?" I asked.

"Your dad can't. It's a gift given only to the women in my family."

"So, Mommy can do it?"

"No, your mom can't do it, not anymore..." she said, pensive. She busied herself by shelling pea pods with impressive speed. When I asked what she meant, she just said that she'd tell me all about it when I got older. I never liked when Grandma said that, because it usually meant I'd never get the answer. However, I also knew that pushing her to tell me never worked. So I let it go—mostly.

"Is this a superpower, like on TV?" I asked, eyes wide in amazement.

"Humph," she replied, dripping with disapproval.

And then she added, "Everyone in our family who's ever called Flashing 'a power' has lived to regret it. Calling it that makes it seem like the world *owes* you a peek into the future. And it does not. Trust me."

"If it's not a power, then what is it?" I asked.

She reflected for a few moments. "It's a gift. Yes, that's exactly what Flashing is. And when someone gives you a gift, what's the first thing you say to them?"

I shrugged. She waited. And then it came to me. "'Thank you."

"Exactly," she replied.

I wanted to know everything there was to know about my gift, but Grandma said I had to wait until I was older for that, too. Luckily, I didn't have to wait too long. I stumbled into an old journal Grandma kept back when she was my age. I found a page where she talked about our gift.

July 1, 1973

Dear Diary,

Today, Mama finally told me the story of how our family got our gift to see a small piece of the future. I'm writing it down here, so I don't forget.

In 1795, the Destrehan Plantation, located in St. Charles Parish, Louisiana, was home to numerous slaves; among them was Abigail Humburg. She was a tiny, frail-looking young woman with fire in her eyes.

It was rumored among the slaves that she had powers that were not of this Earth. She was much beloved by the other slaves because of her ability to cure a number of ailments, using herbal remedies and concoctions.

One night, a prominent friend of the plantation owner, a politician named Clifton Buford, came to visit. Buford took an interest in Abigail. He was given permission to take her into the shed. It had been a peaceful night until Abigail's cries ripped the dark sky open. A violent torrent of rain came down on the land. The winds whipped mercilessly through the tree branches, and lightning struck no less than three times, each time getting closer and closer to the shed.

Buford came out of the shed looking smug. Abigail knew he was going to keep coming back—he had said as much. That night the slaves banded together and helped her escape.

The plantation owner rounded up a group of men and a mob of dogs specially trained to target runaway slaves.

Abigail ran though the bayou alone, so no one could really say what she experienced. But knowing the bayou, many suspected she would have encountered poisonous snakes, alligators, and uneven, slippery slopes.

> *In the heart of the bayou Abigail encountered my ancestor, another escaped slave girl named Santana. Santana saw Abigail and heard the barking of the dogs getting close. Without thinking twice, she rushed to get Abigail and bring her back to the cave where she'd been hiding. Once the dogs were gone, the two emerged out of the small opening.*
>
> *In gratitude, Abigail placed her hands on Santana's forehead. Her whole body began to shake, and her eyes went milky white. She chanted what sounded like some kind of prayer, in a language Santana had never heard before. When it was all done, Abigail told her she'd been given a token of gratitude for her bravery: every female in her bloodline from now on would sometimes glimpse what had yet to come to pass.*
>
> *It's believed that before Abigail died, she was able to bestow similar gifts to other families. I wonder if it's true. Well, if it is, I hope I get to meet them someday.*

When I first read the journal, I dreamed of somehow getting to be as brave as Abigail. I pictured her running through the bayou determined and strong-willed. She decided she wasn't going to let anyone violate her ever again, and she took control. And even though she could have been killed, she sought out freedom. How badass is that?

I often wondered what she'd be like if I were to meet her. I think she'd have the same fire in her eye that Harriet Tubman does in the few pictures I've seen of her.

The gift that Abigail gave our family didn't come with any warnings. There is no way to tell when a Flash will appear or how long the Flash will be. It could appear out of nowhere and last a few seconds or a few minutes. There are two kinds of Flashes: those that are soaked in gray and those that are bathed in red. I can alter the gray visions in some small way and it's no big deal. But the Flashes bathed in red should never be changed.

There's only been one incident that I know of where someone tried to change a red Flash—my great-aunt Betsy. She saw a vision bathed in red of her husband flirting with the housekeeper in the alley of the hotel they were going to on vacation. Aunt Betsy watched as her husband and the housekeeper shared a kiss.

Although she knew her Flash was not to be altered at all, she attempted just that. She canceled the trip. This caused a huge argument. Her husband stormed out and headed for a bar to blow off steam. Later that night, on his way home, a car hit him and severed his spinal cord. He never walked again.

Grandma always brings up her younger sister Betsy's misfortune as a warning to me about misusing my gift. She's repeatedly warned me: One, never treat it as a power. Power is ego. Always treat it as a gift; be grateful. And two, *never* alter a red Flash, no matter what—altering a red Flash will have repercussions for both you and your loved ones. I'm thankful that I've never experienced a red Flash.

There's no pattern to when I'll Flash. I've gone weeks without seeing anything, and sometimes, I'll have one every other day. There's no rhyme or reason. I let the visions play out, unless it can hurt someone, like the shattered glass in the kitchen.

Arlo and my dad are pretty used to my knowing things before they happen. They know I would prefer not to have this ability and that I don't like talking about it. Aunt J knows, too. I had to tell her once she started living with us. I was surprised that I didn't have to convince her that I wasn't lying. But then again, she's really into astrology and healing crystals. So maybe seeing a piece of the future doesn't sound as strange to Aunt J as it might to others.

Grandma has often tried to teach me more about the history of Flashing in our family and ways to safely strengthen my ability. I think she was surprised that I didn't actually want to be able to Flash. The truth is, I'm not a fan of Flashing—it's what got my mom killed.

THREE

LIKE ME, MY MOM DISCOVERED HER GIFT WHEN she was a kid. Growing up, she became more and more fascinated with her ability. Whenever she got a Flash, she'd try to stay in it and see beyond that moment.

Not long after her twenty-first birthday, she started seeing mystics, conjurers, and Voodoo priests, all in an attempt to magnify her vision. She longed to get to the point where she could see years of her life played out before her, not just a moment here and there. My grandma had warned her about tampering with her gift, but she wouldn't listen.

She met with a spiritualist who said he could increase her power by making her a potion. The tonic was toxic and she was sick for weeks after. What's worse is that her gift was gone. It could have been a direct result of the tonic she drank; we're not really sure. For years my mom tried to get it back. That's how she died—she had a car accident on her way to see yet another mystic.

"Really? Tonight of all nights?" Dad says. I pull myself away from thoughts about my mom. It's for the best. I'm always happy when I first see her in my mind's eye, but soon it turns to melancholy.

Dad looks somewhat frazzled when he sees the broken window. I don't think it's that big a deal; the little kids in the neighborhood are always as destructive as they are adorable. The timing sucks, though, since Dad wants everything to be perfect. Luckily for him, Candace texts that she's running late.

That gives us time to tidy up. We put up a plank of wood until we can get the glass fixed. After the boys threw the ball, they all scattered. My dad texts one of their moms, and she tells him to send her the bill. I hear her yell at her son, "Boy, you 'bout to get it!"

A half hour later, we hear a knock on the door. My dad goes to open it, but not before he takes a deep breath and composes himself. While he's at the door, I whisper "Behave" in Arlo's ear. He rolls his eyes, but at least he attempts to smile.

Dad opens the door and hugs Candace.

Candace Becker does not belong here. I don't mean here in our house. I mean she doesn't belong here, in the real world. She belongs in a country music video. I can see it now: she's wearing a flower-print dress, running through a field of wheat, her shiny strawberry-blond hair flowing behind her. The setting sun hits her light-gray eyes and makes them sparkle.

Then comes the part in the video where the love of her life appears and she rushes into his arms. He lifts her up and spins her around. There's no version of this video where the love of her life looks like my dad. I can tell by the look on Arlo's face that he, too, thinks it's an odd pairing.

"Candie, these are the people living with me who eat me out of house and home every day," Dad teases.

Arlo rolls his eyes and addresses Candace. "What Dad means to say is that I'm the son he adores more than life itself. The son he loves so much, it will cause physical pain when I move out of here and head to the East Coast."

Dad shakes his head. "C'mon, man, I already ordered the party balloons for the day you leave," he replies.

Candace elbows my dad in the ribs. "Don't listen to him, Arlo. He brags about you all the time."

Arlo flashes a smile and shakes hands with Candace. "It's nice to meet you."

"And that one over there, the one trying to melt into the paint, is my daughter, Lala," Dad says.

Candace walks over to the corner where I'm standing and beams. "I've heard you play before. You're fantastic!"

"Uh...thanks. When did you hear me play?"

"Well, your dad showed me a video of your last recital. And he's right; you're really talented," she says.

"It's nice to meet you, Candace," I reply, not sure what the right response should be. She seems nice and friendly. And Dad can't take his eyes off her. So that's good, I guess.

"Oh, please, both of you call me Candie. I'm sorry I'm late. Believe it or not, it's still possible to get lost even with GPS," she says.

"It's okay, babe. We're glad you're here," Dad says, placing his hand on her lower back to guide her to the dining room.

Arlo and I look at each other and both silently mouth, *Babe?* That took us by surprise. I'm the first to recover. I signal for Arlo to follow me to the dining room. He comes, but not before he lets out a sigh.

We sit down and begin to eat. Candie comments on how good the food tastes and pushes to know more about Arlo's love of cooking. She asks when he's going to pass on some of that cooking talent to our dad.

"Oh, wait a minute now, I can throw down in the kitchen, too!" Dad says.

✦ 35 ✦

He can't. He sucks at cooking.

Candie rubs his arm gently and says, "That's right, Earl, you can throw down in the kitchen—throw down your apron and call Pizza Hut."

Arlo can't help but laugh, and Dad pretends to be wounded. "Oh, I see, you got jokes!" he says. "Why don't you tell the kids how you fixed the scratch you found on your new car?"

"Hey, nail polish and paint are practically the same thing!" she counters.

We can't help but laugh at the sincerity in her voice. For the next twenty minutes, we talk and banter, and I decide that Candie might be a chill person.

"Your dad tells me your birthdays are tomorrow. You two are turning fifteen! That's exciting. Any big plans?" she asks.

"There's this restaurant I've been wanting to try," Arlo replies. "They fuse Mexican and Italian dishes. It's just outside of Houston, called Rosa Azul."

"That's Arlo's gift. I went the old-fashioned route—cash," I inform her. She nods and says when she was my age, that's what she would have asked for, too.

I'm not saying that I want her to be my mom or anything, but she seems okay. Arlo is having a good time, but

I can tell he's still apprehensive. He keeps looking at Dad to gauge how serious this thing is.

We hear keys in the door.

Arlo, Dad, and I all look at each other, stunned.

Aunt J!

The ease and lightheartedness that was at the table disappears instantly. Dad looks like a kid right before he goes to the dentist. He checks his watch.

"It's only eight thirty," he says to us.

Dad pointing out that Aunt J doesn't get home on Mondays until after ten is pointless. The fact is, regardless of what time she normally comes in, she's here now.

Arlo exhales and puts down his fork.

"Is everything okay?" Candie asks, concern in her eyes.

"Yeah, everything is fine. It's my sister, Janice. She usually works late on Mondays, but I guess not today," Dad replies, failing to hide the stress in his voice.

We hear the door open. Aunt J does what we all do when we first get home—shout needlessly and announce our presence.

"Hey, I'm home. My last client canceled. I swear that Mrs. Rollins works my last good nerve! This is the second appointment she's canceled this month. She thinks I'm playing with her. I'm 'bout to charge next time, you watch..."

We hear her toss her keys in the glass key bowl. Dad stands up. We hear Aunt J's footsteps as she makes her way to us in the dining room. She stops just short. I'm guessing she's at Dad's office, which has become her makeshift bedroom.

She shouts from her room, "Good Lord, that chicken smells too good! Arlo, I know you done saved me some! You better, 'cause after the day I've had... One of my clients, Ms. Edger, went on some fancy vacation with that boyfriend of hers—yes, the one that's half her age. But I ain't mad! I'm glad she's gettin' it!

"Anyway, they were staying at this posh hotel, and that woman had the nerve to use the hotel shampoo! She knows good and well the hotel shampoo ain't for us. How she gonna dump that mess into her 4C hair? And then got dare to come in my shop and ask why her hair so frizzy and dry?

"I swear, when that lady lies down at night, she pray to God to wake up a white woman. But I can't hardly blame her. I know her dad and her brother; two of the most color-struck Negroes I've ever seen. Arlo, go on, make me a plate. I'll be right there." We hear her footsteps. She's coming into the dining room.

"Ah, no, it's okay. I know you're tired. Arlo will bring the food to you. You can stay where you are," Dad says, trying to sound casual about it.

"Nah, I'll come to the table. I ain't seen the kids all day."

We listen to Aunt J marching down the hall and into the dining room.

"Hey! How's everybody—"

The rest of the words die on her lips as she beholds Candace. Aunt J has the same rich, dark complexion her brother has. She loves changing hairstyles, so there's no telling what her hair will look like when she enters. She could be wearing goddess locs, Lemonade braids, or passion twists. But while her hairstyle changes often, her thick and curvy body stays pretty consistent. What I think makes Aunt J so beautiful isn't her shape or her hair; it's the dimple on her left cheek. When you combine that with her chubby baby face and dark eyes, she's stunning.

"Aaah...Janice, this is our guest, my girlfriend—Candace. Candace, this is my sister, Janice," Dad says carefully. I can almost feel him holding his breath.

Candace stands up and extends her hand. Aunt J shoots Dad a look that says in no uncertain terms: *You tried it!*

Dad clears his throat and gives a smile that doesn't reach his eyes. Aunt J turns to Candace and shakes her hand. "Hello, it's nice to meet you. Please sit down."

Dad was relaxed before, but now his posture is stiff and on high alert. Aunt J looks at Arlo and me, as if to ask why we didn't give her a heads-up. We shrug, not sure what else to do. She turns her attention back to Candie.

"I'm sorry I was so loud before. I didn't know we were having company," she says pointedly as she looks across the table at her brother.

"Well, she's here...so let's make her feel welcome," Dad says. His tone is polite and might even be considered warm. But there's no confusion when I read his eyes—he's serious about Aunt J behaving. She returns his glare.

"Earl did tell you that we were dating, didn't he?" Candie asks.

"He told me that he found someone on a dating site. He didn't really go into details," Aunt J replies. She fixes herself a plate of food and places it in front of her. "So, tell me all about yourself, Candace."

"Oh, you can call me Candie."

"I'm happy to call you Candie. So, Candie...tell me all about yourself."

"Um...well. I recently moved here from Atlanta. I was an art major in school, and I always wanted to own my own gallery. And when my realtor told me about a space that was up for sale, I came to take a look and fell in love with the place."

"Candie has a really good eye. There are some beautiful pieces in her gallery," Dad adds.

"I'm surprised you would move here—most people don't really like small towns like ours," Aunt J says.

"This place is so charming. The parks, the sun setting over Morris Bridge. And not to mention the food. That's why it's so unfortunate this whole ugliness is happening with the PCP project. I don't get why some people are so hell-bent on keeping communities divided," Candie says, full of passion.

"I agree one hundred percent, babe," Dad replies.

Aunt J rolls her eyes so quick, I may be the only one who catches it.

"Aunt J put her name down on the waiting list. She might live there," Arlo says.

"*Might*," Dad says, sounding worried. "We need to see how things play out. There are a lot of people who don't want the Manor to open, and there's no telling what they are willing to do to make sure that it doesn't. You should wait a year or two. Now is not the time."

"It's never a good time to piss off bigots, but that's what needs to be done. I signed up, and if they have an opening, I'm going for it. I would have gone to the counterprotest today had I known my client was gonna cancel on me," Aunt J adds.

"You should! I would love to go and protest with you. Just let me know when you plan to go," Candie offers.

Aunt J nods politely but doesn't say anything.

Dad takes out his cell and shows us a video on YouTube. It's a news clip of the protesters arguing with the counter-protesters in front of the Manor. The protesters have signs ranging from flowery, subtle discrimination to outright hate. The counterprotesters hold up signs proclaiming this is America and they have a right to live wherever they want. Both sides are shouting slogans at the top of their lungs, angry and determined to be heard.

One of the white protesters, pissed off and red-faced, shouts the N-word at a woman directly across from him. "What the hell you call me?" the Black woman shouts. Two Black men next to her come to her defense, and soon it's an all-out brawl.

"You see how insane things got? This was a month ago. Now it's getting even worse. You can't be a part of that, Janice. It's too dangerous," Dad says.

"No, it's exactly where I need to be," Aunt J replies. "Look, I know you give money to our causes, and that's great, big brother, but sometimes you need to be on the front line."

"I'm not doing this with you," he says, shaking his head.

Aunt J mutters, "I guess maybe you're too distracted

with other *pursuits* to worry about things like desegregation and fair housing."

"Janice!" he snaps.

She shrugs. "I'm just saying I think it would be nice to show the kids that some things are worth fighting for."

Dad seems like he's trying hard to keep the irritation out of his voice when he says, "You know what I think would be nice—leaving my kids with at least one parent!"

"I'm not saying you should join the protests now that they're getting violent, but she's right, Earl. Things need to get shaken up around here!" Candace says.

"Exactly!" Aunt J agrees. "I love this little town, but folks here can be closed-minded. I don't have to tell you that, Candie—you're dating a Black man in Davey. I can't imagine what people are saying around your neighborhood."

I can't help but feel like the spider is luring the fly into a trap. And judging by the look on my dad's face, he senses the same. Arlo's eyes grow wide as he looks from Candace to Aunt J. He knows something's up.

Candie waves it off. "Oh, I'm used to it by now. People can be such idiots. I've had to deal with that stuff for years."

"Years?" Aunt J asks. "Your last boyfriend was Black, too?"

"He was. His name was Kevin," Candie replies.

"You told me what happened with you two and how you grew apart. I didn't realize he was Black," Dad says.

"Ah, yeah. I thought I mentioned it," Candie replies.

Dad shrugs it off. "It's okay. Who wants to hear all about someone's exes?" He laughs, but it sounds slightly strained.

"Earl and I get looks when we walk around together. But that's nothing. You should have seen how bad it was with my ex before Kevin—Adedayo. He's Nigerian, and the things people would say to him—unbelievable," Candace says, clearly upset.

"So...your last *two* boyfriends have been Black?" Aunt J asks.

Candie thinks for a moment as Dad grinds his teeth and gives his sister the death stare.

"You know what, come to think of it, while I've dated white guys, all of my serious relationships have been with Black men." She laughs and places her hand on top of Dad's hand. "I guess I have a type."

Aunt J addresses Candie but keeps her eyes on Dad. "Hmm, I guess you do."

Arlo whispers in my ear, "RIP Candace and Dad."

Aunt J gets up. "I'm tired. Gonna lie down."

And just before she exits, Aunt J places a hand on Dad's shoulder and says in a biting tone, "Good night, Earl Jr."

Dad closes his eyes, defeated. "Good night, Janice."

Arlo's right: Candace and my dad are over. Everyone knows it.

Candace gazes lovingly into Dad's eyes and gently squeezes his hand.

Well, everyone but Candace...

FOUR

MY DAD SOUNDPROOFED THE BASEMENT YEARS ago so we could turn it into a practice room. I get up every day and play for an hour before school. It feels right that this is the first thing I do on my fifteenth birthday. I'm learning a new piece, and it's basically killing me. But that always happens in the beginning of learning new material.

The alarm on my cell goes off, letting me know I've reached the one-hour mark. I get up from the chair and gently place Grace back in her stand.

I get in the bathroom and turn on the shower. It's nice and hot. I let the water run over me and close my eyes.

Gray spirals flash.

Metal taps metal.

Paint scrapes paint.

Drivers shoot

Bullets made of words.

Target: each other.

Cars.

Cars.

Cars.

Standing

Still.

The Flash is like any other I've had since I was five. I talked to Grandma Sadie last week, though, and she told me that when she turned fifteen, the range of her Flash increased. Before then she was only able to see things that would happen that day, and it has been the same for me. But after her birthday, she was able to see events that didn't occur until weeks later.

Her post-birthday Flashes also had a lot more detail. She said none of these changes happened until the exact time of day she was born. I was born at 3:24 p.m. So there's a good chance my "gift" will get stronger sometime later today. Sigh.

I exit the shower and get dressed. My cell alerts me that I missed a call from Grandma Sadie. She left me a voicemail to say happy birthday. No doubt she left one for Arlo, too. She also sent a picture of my mom I've never seen before. She looks to be about my age. She's standing in front of a green pickup truck, grinning from ear to ear. I add the picture to my phone as the wallpaper.

I'm officially fifteen! There's something about that number that screams adulthood. I know I'm not all the way grown yet, but I'm pretty close.

I look myself over one last time in the mirror. I don't need a Flash. I can see my future as clear as I can see my reflection:

I'll be living in New York City, attending Juilliard. I'll get to play Grace day and night, perfecting my skills. I'll grab coffee with fellow classical musicians; we'll exchange tips on how to avoid nerves before an upcoming performance. We'll sit at all-night cafés, passionately debating which piece is more moving, "The Swan" from *The Carnival of the Animals*, or Elgar's cello concerto.

"La, come get this food before it gets cold," Aunt J shouts from outside my door.

The moment I walk out of my room, I'm greeted by

music. I'm generally surrounded by music every morning. We all get to add songs to the "Morning House" playlist. Dad likes old-school hip-hop, like The Roots. Arlo gets to play all the current hip-hop he wants, so long as it's the clean version. Aunt J is into soul and funk. I'm good with most types of music. Right now, the house is filled with the smooth sound of Earth, Wind & Fire singing "September."

In the kitchen, Aunt J is making our usual birthday breakfast—rabbit-shaped pancakes with chocolate chips for eyes, bacon, and eggs. Arlo is already at the table. Aunt J sets a plate in front of me.

"Auntie, you know we're not little kids anymore. We don't require our foods to be animal-shaped," I remind her.

"So, you don't want it?" she asks, taking the plate away. I quickly pull the plate back. She laughs. "Yeah, that's what I thought." Then she kisses my temple.

I don't even try to argue. Hell, she could make pancakes in the shape of the devil himself and I'd eat them. Arlo is nearly done with his. "I like the hint of cinnamon at the end, Aunt J. Nice little surprise," he says.

"Thank you, chef," Aunt J replies.

Dad walks into the kitchen and gives me a huge bear hug as he wishes me a happy birthday. He squeezes me so hard, it might actually be child endangerment. He goes to hug Arlo, who objects but to no avail.

"Okay, Dad, PDA is one thing, gifts are another," Arlo points out.

Dad tells him he made a reservation for the end of the month at Rosa Azul, the restaurant that Arlo has been hinting he wants to go to for the past year.

I clear my throat and smile politely at my father.

"Very subtle, La. I left your birthday card on my dresser. I wanted to take another look at what I wrote before I handed it to—"

I don't even let my dad finish. I rush into his room. I read the card. It's all gooey, sentimental stuff—and cash. I run back to the kitchen, thank Dad, and dive into my pancakes.

"Last week you said you had trouble with that last section of the new piece. Is it still giving you issues?" he asks me.

I roll my eyes. "That one little section hates me!"

Dad shakes his head. "Nah, you got it. You only need a little more practice, La."

Dad then checks his phone. I'm pretty sure he's reviewing last week's progress report from school. The schools upload all that info for parents to look at, everything from test scores to class projects. Although Arlo and I go to different schools, the progress reports come in the same day.

"Arlo, are you done with your World History report?" Dad asks.

"I'm almost done. But it's not due until the end of next week," Arlo argues.

"Finish tonight, so that by next week, you'll have a chance to improve on it before you have to hand it in," Dad says.

"Dad!" Arlo whines.

"I want that report in my inbox tonight," Dad says. Well, looks like Dad is back to being himself. He turns to me. "La, you're missing a class assignment in Algebra."

"I had really bad cramps that day, and Mrs. Bicker said I didn't have to hand anything in."

"That was last week. Are you feeling better now?" Dad asks.

"Yeah, I guess, but Mrs. Bicker—"

"Mrs. Bicker don't run this house. I do. Hand the assignment in by tomorrow, please."

"Fine," I mutter, then pout.

"Hey, fix your face," Dad warns. I give him a gold-plated smile.

Aunt J goes to her room and comes back with gifts in hand. Arlo gets what he's been dying for—red suede Nike Air Force Ones with black pythons. And I get a gorgeous sterling silver treble clef pendant with my birthstone. Both Arlo and I squeal like little kids and thank her.

"We need to leave here in five minutes or else," Dad says. He's always been the timekeeper in the mornings. He takes me to school, and Aunt J, who works near Arlo's school, drops him off.

"You both need jackets," she says. "It's gonna warm up later, but it's chilly now. Go get 'em."

Arlo goes to get his jacket; I gobble down the rest of my food and grab a light jacket from the hall closet.

Dad waits until Aunt J is out of earshot and then asks, "So... now that you two have met Candace, what do you think of her? She told me she really liked you two."

Arlo and I exchange a look, each begging the other to speak first. *Fine, I'll go.* "Candace was nice. We had a good time last night."

"I'm glad. And you, Arlo?" Dad asks.

"Ah, yeah. She was cool," Arlo says, avoiding eye contact.

"Good," Dad says as Aunt J joins us. He goes for his car keys, and then I remember my Flash.

"Dad, there's gonna be a fender bender that's gonna stall traffic. Let's take a different route to school today."

He nods. We all pile out of the house.

"Everyone have a great day. Love y'all. Be safe," Aunt J says as she gets into her car with Arlo.

I get in with my dad, and we go the long way like I suggested. While I'm fiddling with the radio, a traffic report comes in about how backed up the street that we normally drive on is. Dad and I exchange a knowing glance. Guess the fender bender happened.

"La, remember when you first started to Flash, and I told you I didn't want to know what you saw?"

I'm taken off guard, because we almost never even say the word *Flash*, let alone talk about it. But judging by Dad's tone, he seriously wants to chat about my visions.

"I remember."

"Well, I still don't want to know the *details*, but... I need to know if you saw anything about me and Candace. Did you get a Flash about us at all? Good or bad?"

There's desperation in his voice that breaks my heart a little. "No, Dad, I didn't see anything."

I don't need a Flash to know what will happen with you two.

Dad knows it, too. But knowing something and being able to say it out loud are two different things. It was two whole years before I could actually say the words "My mom died" out loud.

We're about two miles away from my school when we pass Millwood Manor. Since this isn't our normal route, I don't usually see the building that has caused all this drama in Davey.

"When did that happen?" I ask my dad, pointing to the bay window in the front of the building. Someone had hurled a brick though the glass.

"I don't know. I drove by here yesterday and it was fine," Dad says. There are two cops asking people questions and taking notes. Meanwhile, a third cop is placing caution tape around the shattered glass.

God, I gotta get out of this town...

FIVE

DAD DROPS ME OFF, AND I STAND IN FRONT OF the school and look on as a sea of kids enters. I think it'd be odd for most people to go to a school where only five other people look like them. But for me, it's become the norm. There are very few Black faces in the classical competitions I've entered throughout the years. And on the rare occasion that I do see a Black face, there's an unmistakable sense of relief. I make eye contact and we do the nodding thing. It feels nice not to be the only one there.

I've been at Ross Academy for over a year now, and the school building still blows me away. On the outside this place looks more like a cathedral than a school. Everything about its architecture is bougie and undeniably impressive, from its ornate archways to its stained glass mosaic windows.

I enter, and, as always, the Confederate flag is the first thing that waves hello to me. It's one of many Confederate flags in the school. I say hi to a few of the kids I know from classes. But for the most part, I keep to myself as I walk toward my locker. I can't stand how expensive this school is, but to be real, it's a musician's dream. We have state-of-the-art everything, from practice rooms to recording studios, and even two concert halls.

Despite the above, don't get it twisted—this school is very much like any other high school. There are cliques, disgruntled staff, and the unmistakable scent of anxiety. Where this school does differ from others is the level of intensity when it comes to classwork—if it relates to our major.

We have academics in the morning, then gym or whatever PE class we are required to take. But afternoon is when the student body comes alive. It's the part of the day that's reserved for music. The competition among us is intense to say the least. When it comes to our chosen instruments, we don't play around.

I open my locker, expecting yet another flyer from Black Alliance. And sure enough, there it is. This one is bright blue. I read it, although I know it says the same thing as before: JOIN US OR DIE. Okay, it doesn't say that, but it might as well.

"Zora got you again, huh?" my best friend, Ruby, asks as she walks up to me. Rue is short and thick, with a dark brown complexion and big, expressive eyes. Her silk-pressed jet-black hair is long, and there's never a strand out of place. As always, she's dressed to impress. She has a closet of clothes any fashionista would sell their soul to get a peek at.

Rue is a coloratura. That's an uppity way of saying her voice is the highest of all the sopranos. She's an opera singer, learning to master trills, agile runs, and leaps. It's tough, because while doing all of the above, a coloratura must also be lighter and faster than all the other sopranos.

"Where does she find the time?" I ask.

Rue laughs and says, "You could just agree to join, you know. I love Black Alliance."

"Yeah, I know," I reply with very little enthusiasm.

"So sign up," she says, not for the first time.

"Can we reschedule this debate? It is my birthday, after all," I point out.

"Is it? I forgot," she says, doing a horrible acting job.

"No, you didn't."

She gives me a devious smile. "Hell no. I'm not gonna forget my girl!"

"Okay, but remember we had a deal."

"I know, I know," she replies, rolling her big eyes.

Rue's loaded. Her family is one of only a handful of Black families that live on the north side. They live in a gated community called Belle Gardens. She has one or two cool neighbors, but the community at large is full of people who make an art form out of microaggressions.

Her family has been rich for generations. It started in the early nineteen hundreds, when they created a skincare product called Gold & Honey. I can't lie—their products are top of the line. I can't afford them, but Rue hooks me up.

"I wish you were there last night. You could have helped me fake a heart attack or something to get away from Nana Dee. She and my grandpa came by yesterday—unannounced."

"Argh, I'm so sorry!" I reply, rubbing her shoulder.

Most of Rue's family is cool. Yeah, they can be a little stuck-up, but all in all, they are still pretty nice. There's only one person in her family that grates on my last nerve—her Nana Dee. Argh! That woman is just the worst! She has five grandchildren total. And she treats all of them very well—except Rue.

The fact is, she doesn't like that Rue is several shades

darker than the rest of her grandchildren. She's always trying to get Rue to try some "beauty cream," only for Rue to read the label and discover that it's really glorified bleaching cream.

Anytime Rue goes to visit, Nana Dee is always yelling at her to get out of the sun. I've been invited to family dinners and have seen her be loving and attentive to her other grandchildren, all the while ignoring Rue. She's a spiteful, brittle, dried-up twig. And I pray for the day the wind carries her colorist ass far away from my best friend.

"Did she say anything horrible to you? Are you okay?" I ask.

Rue shrugs. She acts like it's no big deal that her nana is always throwing shade. But I think she'd love it if, just once, her nana looked at her with the same pride with which she looks at her other grandchildren.

Honestly, I don't know how anyone can be mean to Rue. She's a kind, ratchet-music-loving goofball with an A average. When I'm down, she sings hip-hop songs to me in her opera voice, and I die laughing. You have not lived until you've heard a Megan Thee Stallion track remixed into an operetta. That's the one thing even Nana Twig can't deny: my girl's voice. Rue is the best singer in the school. Period.

"On second thought, let's not even talk about Nana. I'm glad she only came for dinner and isn't spending the whole week with us. Now, about your gift..."

"Rue, remember, we made a deal: nothing too pricey."

"Wait, I don't remember a deal," she lies.

I fold my arms across my chest and give her a look. Last year we struck a deal as far as birthdays go: We do not spend more than fifty bucks on each other. How crusty would it look if Rue got me a tennis bracelet, and on her birthday, I handed her coupons to Popeyes?

"Okay, fine. Yes, yes. I remember the deal," she says.

"Good, now what did you get me?" I ask way too eagerly.

She hands me a long, narrow black box, the kind that a necklace would come in. I open it and scream!

"Ladies, perhaps some decorum on this fine Tuesday morning?" our music theory teacher scolds us as she walks by.

"Yes, Mrs. Belle," Rue and I mumble in unison. Mrs. Belle is Cruella de Vil with a hint of Dolores Umbridge from Harry Potter. That is to say, she basically sucks. We wait for her to pass before we get back to screaming—in a low whisper.

"Rue, you really got us tickets to the Houston Symphony to see the Jacqueline Mary du Pré tribute?"

"Yes, because I'm that amazing," she gloats.

I yank her toward me and give her the biggest hug I've ever given anyone. It's only when we pull apart that reality sets in.

"Hold up. There's no way these tickets were only fifty bucks," I accuse her.

"Girl, I am wounded. How you gonna doubt me like that?" she says, pretending to be emotionally distressed. I point to the spot on the ticket where the price is clearly displayed.

She looks away. And then, before I can scold her, she quickly changes the topic.

"How did the dinner with your dad's new girl go? Did you get a Flash about what she'd be like before she came over?"

Rue is the only person outside my family that knows I can Flash. In the beginning, she thought I had lost my mind. But when things I said would happen actually happened, she started to come around.

"I didn't get a Flash about meeting her."

"So you had to go in blind. Got it. Did you like Candace? Did you hate her? 'Cause I can hate her right along with you! You know how I do"

I laugh and start to give her a recap, but then the bell

rings. I promise to fill her in later, and we hurry to first period.

I see Zora in my second and third period classes. I know she's just waiting to ambush me again. Thankfully, I manage to rush out of both classes before she can approach me and make her pitch. But it's futile, because after lunch, as I go rushing to my locker, who is right behind me?

"Sis, I've been looking for you," she says with her usual chill vibe. She's wearing vintage tan corduroy jeans that flare out at the bottom and a black Jimi Hendrix T-shirt. She combines that with suede boots and square, vintage pink sunglasses. And, as always, she's sporting a bunch of rings on her fingers and one in her nose. This outfit would look ridiculous on anyone else. But on Zora, it's fire! I think it's her air of "unbothered" that allows her to wear just about anything and make it work.

"Did you see the flyer I put in your locker?" she asks.

"Ah, yeah, I did. I like that new logo."

"Thanks! Are we gonna see you this afternoon? Black Alliance starts at three fifteen," she says, filled with hope and enthusiasm.

I decide right then to rip off the Band-Aid. I mean, how many ways can I politely turn her down? I need to be straight up, or I'll have collected a forest's worth of flyers by the end of the school year.

"To be honest, Zora, Black Alliance is not really my thing, you know what I mean?" I admit.

"Nah, sis, run that back."

Okay, so how do I say this and not sound like a complete jerk?

"I don't think I'm a good fit for your club," I say gently.

She arches one eyebrow and side-eyes me so hard, Arlo would be impressed.

"Yeah, I know I'm Black, and so it's supposed to be a natural fit, but..."

She leans in and waits patiently for me to finish my thought. *Argh! Screw this!*

"Look, I don't want to be in your club because I don't want to be reminded every hour of the day that racism is real. I got it. What I need is to play brilliantly so I can get the hell out of this little town and go to New York, where there won't be all of this race stuff!"

I'm not sure how I expected her to react, but it wasn't with a big smile. It's more of a smirk.

Hold up, is she laughing at me?

"Zora, what's so funny?" I ask.

"That's the plan? Get out of Davey? Bigger town, larger capacity for tolerance?"

I shrug. "Makes sense to me."

"You don't think there's gonna be race 'stuff' in New York? Chicago? Atlanta? Are you looking for a racism-free state, sis?"

"I know that other places have issues. I'm saying it won't be as bad as it is here. But to get to New York, I need to focus. So, no clubs. Besides, you have, like, twenty people in the club already. Plus, you have the only three Black guys in the school, Rue, and yourself. Does it really matter if the last remaining Black student doesn't join?"

"Yeah, it matters! If we go to admin together, all six of us, in addition to the rest of the members, we might get a meeting with the principal. That's the first step in trying to get that flag down."

"And then what? Are we gonna get the flag down at other schools? Get it down from the post office and all the other public buildings? Don't you see, Zora? It doesn't matter. It's always gonna be something. If I had ten lives, I would dedicate one to ending racism everywhere. But it turns out I have just one! And I'm sorry, but I don't want to use it to help Black Alliance make some gesture that won't have any lasting effect."

She coils one of her locs around the tip of her index finger and tilts her head slightly as she thinks. When she finds her words, she stops coiling and looks me dead in the eyes. When she speaks, her tone is void of the usual ease and self-confidence.

"I saw you play two years ago, in the Monroe Competition."

My stomach flips and my mouth goes dry. "I didn't place, but still, I played pretty well," I mumble.

She smiles. "Sis, you killed it! You outplayed everyone in that concert hall, and you know it. But the three judges, they were never going to pick you no matter how well you played. And at the end, when everyone lined up to shake hands with the judges, one of them skipped you completely. He couldn't even bring himself to shake your hand."

The details of that day two years ago come back to me in a rush. I can still feel my cheeks grow hot from the embarrassment of having the judge walk past me. It pissed me off so much, not because I didn't win but because music was supposed to be the one place where all that race BS didn't matter. It took me a while to shake off the experience and get back to Grace.

"Look, I thought I should have won, too, or at least placed. But everyone thinks they play the best. I could have lost fair and square," I insist.

"That's just it, sis—you'll never know. How much of it was the way you played and how much was what you looked like? Everyone else who was in the competition had one job: play. But you had two jobs: play music and play detective. Look for clues, read the judges' body language, spot the signs. Look for any indication that they might be judging you on something other than the way you play. It's...exhausting. I saw the look on your face after it was all over. You looked like all of us do the first time we realize music won't save us from real life."

Her words make my jaw tighten and my heart race. She shouldn't have brought up the Monroe Competition. I was grateful that it was the one time my dad couldn't come to see me play. When it was over, I felt like someone had disassembled me and put my pieces back together in the wrong order.

"Look, I don't want to be in your stupid club. Get over it," I reply harshly.

I know she doesn't deserve that. It's not her fault she's better at being a Black girl than I am. It's not her fault that nothing in me is as courageous as Santana was back on the bayou.

"Okay, sis. I won't hit you up to join us anymore. But when you leave this town and go somewhere that doesn't have *any* form of racism, institutional or otherwise, ping me your location. I'd like to get to this magical place, too."

SIX

When the school day is over, all the students usually scatter to one of three places: private rehearsal rooms for more practice, after-school clubs, or the local hangout—Bonnie Blue. It's a hamburger place with sinfully good fries and delicious burgers.

I would normally be in a rehearsal room playing, but Rue is missing Black Alliance so she can take me out to eat for my birthday. I had to make her promise to stick to a budget, and after way too much back and forth, she agreed. We both get our stuff and stand by my locker; the school halls are mostly empty.

The plan is for Rue and me to wait until 3:24 and see

what, if any, changes occur to my ability to Flash. I set an alarm on my cell and recount to Rue today's encounter with Zora and last night's dinner.

When I'm done telling her about last night, there's only sixty seconds until it's time. Rue and I exchange a nervous glance and hold each other's hand.

My cell dings. It's 3:24.

Nothing happens.

We both roll our eyes at how needlessly dramatic we were being.

Suddenly, my body goes stiff. My head jerks up toward the ceiling. A white film coats my eyes. I'm shaking and disoriented, like a kitten caught in the eye of a storm.

A flash of gold spiraling.

A person bathed

in moonlight

and shadow.

Wristwatch

Glows.

Green.

Risk watch.

Lost.

Knocking.

Tap

Tap

Tap

On white oak door.

Owner appears

Loads fear

Into cannon.

Fire.

Life

Bleeds

Red stream.

Black

Body

Lies

Still.

    I lose all sense of time and don't come back into myself until I feel the sensation of being shaken. Rue has one hand on each of my arms.

    "La, come back! La!"

I'm gasping for air the first few seconds after I return to my senses. Rue asks if I'm okay. I tell her what I saw: A Black boy, about our age, knocking on a white door. He's wearing an Apple Watch. The date is seven days from now. At 7:07 p.m. The homeowner is an elderly white man. He opens the door and shoots the boy.

"*Dead?*" she shouts. A few students walking down the hall holding oboes turn and look at us. "What? Keep walking, oboes!" Rue orders them.

They shake their heads at her and turn the corner.

"Lala, are you sure the boy was dead? Like, *dead* dead?" she asks, her voice cracking.

"Yes!" I shout.

"Maybe he's just injured," she suggests.

"Rue, I felt the life drain from him. His body was still and hollow. Like there was nothing there anymore."

"Okay, who's the kid? Do you know him? We have to stop him from knocking on the door," she says, panicking.

There are about a hundred questions running through my mind. But I force myself to stop and take a breath. And Rue does the same thing.

"Let's start over from the top, La. You saw this boy from behind, so you don't know what his face looks like?"

"No. I could only see the back of his head clearly, but the farther down I looked, the more shadow there was.

The only other thing I could make out aside from time and date on his watch was his red sneakers."

"That doesn't really tell us much," she says, deflated.

And then it hits me like lightning. "There was a bright silver logo on the back of his jacket. I know that logo; it's the new one from Black Alliance!"

"Good, so we know it's someone from the club. But there're three Black guys in Black Alliance—which one?" Rue asks.

"I guess whichever one of them has an Apple Watch?" I reply.

"La, you have an Apple Watch; so do I and basically most of the school."

She's right. Apple Watches are everywhere around here. Ruby starts to count on her fingers. "I don't know. There's Alex, who we know you have a thing for—"

"Rue!"

"I know, I know. That's not the point. Sorry. There's Ford—the guy who thinks he's God's gift to all girls. And Wes, the nerd who's been bringing a briefcase to school since, like, the first grade."

"The boy in the vision has dark brown skin. But that doesn't help because all three of the guys have similar skin tones and builds. Do you know them well enough to guess which of them I might have seen?"

"Sorry, I don't. We hang out as a group, but we're not tight like that, one on one," Ruby says.

"I need to talk to my grandma. She'll know what I should do."

I call Grandma Sadie on video. "There's my grandbaby! Oh, and my Rue-Rue," she says, beaming with pride. But she takes one look at our faces and her light tone changes. "What's wrong?"

"Grandma, you have to help me!"

"Okay, calm down. Tell me what happened. Was it a new Flash? Was it stronger than the others, like I predicted?"

"Grandma, it was awful," I reply as the weight of what I saw starts to set in. Rue holds my hand as I recount everything in my vision and how much time I think we have until it happens. Grandma listens closely.

"La, are you sure he's dead in the Flash?" Grandma asks.

I nod. "Someone in this school is going to die. You have to help me stop it, Grandma."

"I will. But first, what color was the Flash? Was it gray? If so, we should be able to stop this from happening. If it's red, then we won't be able to change anything without risking something happening to you or a loved one."

I'm relieved that finally there's some good news. "The Flash wasn't red, so it can be changed."

"So your Flash was gray?" Grandma asks.

"Well, actually... It was odd. The Flash wasn't red or gray. I was so freaked out by what I saw when the boy hit the ground, I forgot that part."

"What color was it?"

I think back. "Gold. Yeah, the Flash was gold."

"Are you *sure*? Lala, this is very important," Grandma says.

"Yes, I'm sure."

Grandma begins to tear up and looks up to the heavens. And then she nods to herself, clearly overwhelmed. "It's gold. The Flash is gold, baby," she says, placing her palms together as if in prayer.

"Grandma, what does that mean? And why didn't you tell me that gold Flashes were a thing?" I ask.

Grandma wipes her eyes and steadies herself. "I never told you about them because they're so rare."

"Grandma, what does it mean?" I push.

"There's only been two other times a gold Flash has appeared. The first was in 1810. Santana's daughter Lena was fifteen. She saw a gold Flash of a slave boy secretly being taught to read by his owner. She wanted to warn the boy to stop, because she feared learning to read would get him killed."

I want to ask questions, but I restrain myself. I need to

hear this, so I nod and listen. But I can't help the churning in my stomach. Some part of me knows it's headed for something I won't like.

Grandma goes on, "But her mother had cautioned her that not all Flashes were meant to be changed. So she never approached the boy. After having learned to read, the boy was able to expand his mind. Twenty-one years later, in 1831, that boy grew up to be the leader of the first and only successful slave revolt in US history."

"Wait, Santana's daughter had a gold Flash about the boy who would grow up to become Nat Turner?" I ask.

"Yes. But at the time, all she knew was that there was a little boy whose path should not be altered. And it wasn't just that he staged a rebellion. The slave owners loomed over the plantation with the audacity of gods. Turner pierced their armor and allowed the slaves to see...gods can bleed," Grandma says.

"And the second gold Flash, who saw it? And what happened?" I ask.

"The second gold Flash would not come until over one hundred years later. November first, 1955. Your great-aunt Eloise was fifteen. She saw a Flash surrounded by gold. And in it stood a wary black woman waiting for public transportation to get home. One month later, that woman was arrested for refusing to move to the back of the bus."

Rue shouts, "Rosa Parks!"

"Exactly. Lala, a red Flash can alter the destiny of your personal life and the lives of people you know and love. But a gold Flash shows an event that will alter the fate of our people. There's a change coming! There'll be new laws, new protections, and safety measures for our people. This is the movement that will put a stop to casual killing of unarmed Black children. The new movement is here, baby, it's here!" Grandma says with tears in her eyes.

"But what about the boy in my Flash? How do I save him?" I ask.

Her face falls. Grief and sadness crease the corners of her mouth; tears fall freely from her troubled face. Her prolonged silence is unbearable. I need her to tell me that what I'm thinking isn't really what I think I'm hearing.

"Grandma, c'mon! Please! How do I save this boy?"

"You don't," she says gravely.

"What? No! No." I rage, turning away from the screen.

"Lala—"

"I will not let this kid die!"

"Baby, listen to me very carefully. When Rosa Parks refused to sit in the back of the bus, millions of Black lives were changed. If you alert this boy to his fate, you'll stop the next nationwide Civil Rights Movement."

"You're saying I should let this kid die?"

"I'm saying that on the morning she's supposed to make history, you can't tell Rosa Parks to hail a cab."

"Please...this is a boy's life." I can't see through my tears. My shaking hands can barely hold the phone.

"I'm sorry this Flash chose you. I really am. I can't imagine how hard this is for you, La."

"I can't just stand by. I have to help this kid." I sob.

"Lala, you will have to make a choice: save the boy or save the movement."

SEVEN

MY GRANDMOTHER'S WORDS WRAP AROUND ME like a blanket. The more I try to break free, the tighter it gets. I'm both too hot and too cold at the same time. The ground beneath me is beginning to sway, and the phone in my hand feels like it weighs a ton. I lower my hand and lean against the wall for support. I'm almost certain there's no air left in my body, so it's impressive that I have yet to pass out.

"Lala? Baby, where are you? I am only seeing the hallway. Are you there?" Grandma asks.

I want to answer her, but I feel bile in the back of my throat; I'm pretty sure if I open my mouth, I'll throw up. Rue gently takes the phone from me and talks to Grandma.

"Grandma Sadie, she's here leaning on the wall."

"Is she all right?"

"I'm fine," I reply in a whisper.

"Well, I'll be able to see for myself when I get over there. I got to set my eyes on you and your brother."

"You're coming to Davey?" I ask.

"Yes. I don't want you to go through this on your own."

"While you're here, can you help me bring up the Flash so I can figure out where this all takes place?"

"La, it doesn't matter where it's taking place, you need to let it happen."

"I have to know, Grandma. Even if it can't be stopped. I should know who is going to die and when and where. Please? I don't want to try and expand my Flash on my own."

I don't need to tell Grandma what can happen when someone in the family tries to tamper with their gift without a guide. My mom is a cautionary tale. And I know Grandma doesn't want a repeat of that. So even though she's reluctant, she agrees to help me try to explore my Flash.

"I'm going to catch the first flight out, and I should be there later tonight," she says.

"But what about you and Dad?"

"Don't worry about me and your father. You just focus

on the fact that there is finally going to be some relief for our people. You don't know how my heart aches every time I turn on the news and some poor child has lost their life just because they look like you and Arlo. I can't tell you what this will mean for us as a people," she says.

"Grandma, I get it, but that would mean I have to be okay standing back and letting a kid get shot in the chest! How can I do that? And how can you ask me to?" I reply, wiping the fresh wave of tears streaming down my face.

"I know. But that boy in your vision is one kid. Get online and see how many kids have been casually killed in the past few years for one racist reason or another."

"Grandma, I know there have been instances of that happening. I'm not naive. But—"

"Instances? No, baby, it's so much more than that. I'm sending a link to a site that has been reporting on kids who have been hurt or killed for no other reason than the fact that they are Black. Keep in mind, these are only the ones we know about."

My cell dings and a link pops up on the screen, just above the video of Grandma.

"You got it?" she asks.

I nod. "Grandma—"

"I have to go book my flight, baby. Do not talk to any

more people about this Flash. The more people who know, the harder it will be to keep the vision from being tampered with. Remember, we can't change anything."

"Okay..." I mutter weakly.

"Click the link, Lala. I know you'll come to agree with me. I love you." And before I can say anything else, the screen goes black.

Rue and I look at each other. Neither of us knows what to do next. My cell dings again, reminding me that Grandma sent me a link. Rue and I look at the screen together; the letters and numbers in the link are in bright blue, waiting impatiently for us to click. I know if I click, it will make me feel worse. And yet that's clearly the next step.

"You ready?" Rue asks.

No.

"Yes," I say out loud.

I click the link, thinking it's going to be a list of slain Black folks who were shot while unarmed. I'm wrong. It's a video. It's two minutes long and features various clips from police dash cams and cell phone footage from witnesses.

The first clip is of some guy, a few years older than us, running away from an officer. That's followed by a sharp "bang" sound. The kid hits the ground.

I drop my cell and run to the bathroom. I barely make it inside the stall before I throw up the entire contents of my stomach.

I didn't think any part of my birthday would be spent puking in the girls' bathroom, but here I am. When I'm done, I open the stall door and Rue is waiting for me.

"Feeling better?" she asks, concern carved into her face.

"No. But I think I'm done vomiting, so... there's that," I reply as I walk over to the sink and wash my mouth out. The cold water feels good on my skin, so I splash my face and my neck. Rue hands me some paper towels and a mint from her designer backpack. I'm not surprised; Rue is a walking Walgreens. She prides herself on having any and everything that might be needed throughout the day. But something tells me there's nothing in her Prada backpack that can make this better.

We walk out of the bathroom and make our way back to my locker. I feel as empty as my stomach does. And I also feel fragile, as if the gentlest breeze could knock me over.

"You don't look too good. Should we get you something to eat?" Rue asks.

The thought of eating makes my stomach queasy all

over again. "I think I'm gonna skip food for now, and maybe the rest of my life," I groan.

"We should get out of here. Get some air. C'mon, let's get your stuff."

When we make it to my locker, whatever will I had to stay upright is gone. I slide down the front of my locker and wrap my arms around my knees. My tears flow freely; I don't even try to hold them back.

Rue joins me on the shiny floor, puts her head on my shoulder, and says, "It's gonna be okay, La." I don't need to look at her to know she's crying, too; I can hear the tears in her voice. We sit there for a while; we can hear the distant playing of violins and harps. All the rooms are soundproof, but sometimes students leave the door open, just to get some air or show off how well they are playing.

"I wish it wasn't happening so soon," Rue says.

"Time won't make this better. One week or two years from now, I still know that someone will be killed."

"So you are going to take your grandmother's advice and let it play out?" Rue says.

The question makes me feel sick all over again. "I don't know."

"Try not to worry. I'm sure Grandma Sadie's gonna find a way to help you make this choice."

I roll my eyes and lean my head back against the locker door.

"What is it?" Rue asks.

"I love my grandma, but I don't think she's coming to help me choose. I think she's coming to make the decision for me."

"Letting your grandma pick out your outfit or your boyfriend would be a terrible idea. But deciding the fate of all Black people in this country sounds like something I'd be more than happy to pass on to Grandma Sadie or someone else."

"Yeah, but..." I turn to face her. "It's *my* decision to make, Rue."

"La, how can you—"

The classroom door across the hall from us opens. A surge of students comes out; the first to exit is Zora, followed closely by the rest of Black Alliance.

"Rue, I remember the day my teacher said I was done with three-quarter cellos. He said I was tall enough to handle a full cello. I was so excited. My dad asked me to pick a full cello out of a catalog. He didn't get that I had to meet the cello in person. I had to get to know her. That's what I have to do here," I say, staring at the energetic group of kids as they joke around and gather in clusters. "Ruby, I need to get to know the three guys."

"Nope. Bad idea," she says, shaking her head with certainty.

"What? Why?" I ask.

"It will make it harder."

"I know, but *shouldn't* it be hard? Ruby, we're talking about ending some guy's life—shouldn't I at least know something about him? Has he ever been in love? What are his hopes and dreams? What's been the biggest disappointment in his life so far? How can I sentence someone to death and not even bother to find out who he really is?"

She puts her hand on my shoulder. "La, you didn't choose this for them. The universe or God or whoever did. Not you. We need to blame that hateful old man who takes the shot."

I look over at the group of students hanging out and talking. My eyes land on Alex, one of the best violinists in our sophomore year. Usually I don't do the thing where I fantasize about a guy all day, every day. That space is filled with music instead. But when I see Alex, I can't help the butterflies that take flight in my stomach.

I bumped into him in the hall once. We were both wearing short-sleeved shirts, and our elbows touched. I'm pretty sure I heard music. Granted, I'm in a music school, but this was different. This melody was the kind that only comes from making contact with your crush.

His brown eyes are so dark, they look almost black. He sits next to me sometimes in music theory, and when the sun hits his face, I can see flecks of amber in them. Oh, and not to mention his lips—they look so...kissable.

Whenever I think about my first kiss, my stomach does a flip. But when I think about that first kiss being with Alex, it also makes my knees weak.

He's looking at me!

I quickly avert my eyes. My face gets warm and my heart is racing. I look over at the other two guys. Wes has a skin tone slightly more bronze than the others, and he has light-green eyes.

Wes doesn't really say much, at least not in any of the classes I've had with him. Although he's shy, when he has a saxophone in his hands, his confidence is otherworldly. I guess he's a new fusion of nerdy coolness.

The other Black guy in our school is Ford. He has a charming, crooked smile. He's leaning on the wall with one hand placed above a girl's head and the other in his pocket. I don't know how much practice it took to perfect that "sexy lean" thing he's doing. And it seems to have been worth it—that girl is eating it up.

It's easy to see why he's so popular. He's fit and dangerously handsome. And even more impressive is how insanely good he is with his instrument. I've seen him play piano during school concerts; it gave me goose bumps.

"You were right, Rue—all three of them have Apple Watches," I say.

"So, what now?"

"Look, I'm not sure what I'm going to do. But I am sure that getting to know a little bit about these guys is the right thing to do," I insist.

She shakes her head sadly. "Then let's do this. C'mon, before they leave," Rue says, getting up to head over to the group. That's one thing about my BFF: if she's with you, she's with you all the way.

We run over to the Black Alliance group congregating in the hall.

"Hi, Zora!" I say with a big smile.

Zora is perplexed by my cheerful greeting. "Oh, what's up?" she says curtly.

I elbow Rue and try to get her to help me melt some of the ice from Zora's tone.

"Z, sorry I missed the meeting. It's Lala's birthday and I wanted to celebrate with her. And do you know what she wanted to do? Hang out with you guys in Black Alliance."

"Lala wants to do what?" Zora asks in disbelief.

"I'm sorry about before. I shouldn't have dismissed this club without first giving it a chance," I admit.

"To be real, I wasn't feelin' your vibe earlier today. But I'm thinking maybe I was wrong. It's your life, sis; you gotta walk the path that feels most righteous to you," Zora says.

"That's just it—her path might be with our club," Rue says.

Zora looks me over suspiciously. I join in and hope my voice doesn't betray the anxiety coursing through me. "I'm doing an extra-credit paper about life in Davey and what it's like to live in a sundown town. Rue suggested I interview some of the members from your club."

Zora thinks for a beat and then says, "Okay, I could rock with that." She starts to call out names of various members of the group to be interviewed.

"I actually know which members I want to speak to— if that's cool with you," I say. "Lets start with the three Black guys in the group, and next week I will get the Black female perspective. If that's okay. And, of course, I'd talk to non-Black members as well, down the line." I hope I sound convincing.

"Before I agree to this, I need you to sign our petition. We have over one hundred names already, but it won't have as much power unless all the Black students sign it.

There are only six of us, but it looks bad if we all don't appear to be on the same page," Zora says.

She's no fool. She knows I want the interviews and that she can leverage that to get what she needs. I'm not mad. I get why she's the president.

"Okay, I'll sign," I reply. She takes out her cell and hands her phone to me. I see a screen featuring the petition she referred to. I digitally sign my name.

"I'm surprised you're not using this to get me to join the group," I admit.

"Sis, I don't want to force you. I'm hoping that getting to know some of our members will help persuade you to at least attend a meeting and see what it's all about. I'm also hoping nice swag will sway you," she says. She goes back inside the classroom and comes out with a black jacket with the Black Alliance logo on it.

"This is the last one. And it's in your size," she says, handing it to me.

"Thanks, but aren't these for club members?" I ask.

"I think it's only a matter of time before you become one," she says. "Just promise to keep an open mind."

I agree to her terms and take the jacket.

Zora tilts her chin toward me. "You can start with Wes right after school tomorrow," she says, then leaves before I confirm if that time works for me. I don't think she cares if it does or not. I should be annoyed, but I can't help but marvel at how certain she is of herself. Zora leaves me in awe and slightly envious.

As the group walks away, I swear I see Alex take one last look at me. But I could be wrong; it's a quick glance.

"So, starting tomorrow, I'll find out as much as I can about all three," I tell Rue.

She looks at me. "La, I understand why you're doing this. But fair warning, you're making a difficult thing nearly impossible."

EIGHT

RUE AND I DECIDED TO RESCHEDULE MY BIRTH-day meal for another time, since eating was the last thing on our minds. Instead, we walk outside and wait for our rides. While we were in school, the temperature started to drop. And now there are gray clouds that look like they're about to burst open. I can smell that the rain is on its way. It feels good to have the cold air hit my face. I close my eyes and pretend I just had a regular day at school.

I open my eyes, and that dream quickly fades.

"So...how was your day?" I ask Rue. We laugh in spite of ourselves. We know nothing is funny but need to laugh regardless.

When Rue's driver comes to pick her up, she asks him to wait until my dad comes so that I won't be waiting outside, alone. Ten minutes later my dad honks the horn and I hug Rue goodbye. She holds me extra tight today, and I'm really glad she does.

"This storm is coming out of nowhere. I don't want it to catch us on the road—c'mon, Small Fry, get in," Dad calls out the window. I wave to Rue and get in.

"You're really quiet over there," he says after a few minutes of silence from me. "What's wrong? You look like you're carrying the weight of the whole world."

Nope, just the Black part.

"Dad, did you go to any Black Lives Matter marches?" I ask.

"Of course. It was me, your mom, your aunt J, and your grandma. You and Arlo were too young to come with us."

"Do you think the marches made a difference—I mean in a big way. Did it make things better? Or about the same?"

"Wow, um... I think the marches did make a difference. It's important to stand up for the things you believe in. It was starting to feel like open season on Black folks, especially the young ones. That reckoning was long overdue. Is this for class? Do you have a history assignment due? I don't remember seeing that on your progress report this morning."

"No, I was just curious," I reply, looking out the window. The difference in the weather is now night and day. This morning was sunny although somewhat chilly. But now, the color has seeped out of Davey and left us with a canvas of gray on gray: gray, brooding clouds hanging from gray, murky skies. I drift off, and a wave of thoughts hits me, threatening to pull me into the undertow and drown me.

What if Grandma is wrong and nothing happens after this kid dies—no movement, no revolution—what then? Will this kid have died for nothing?

The undercurrent is strong. It latches on to me, pulling me down deeper and deeper into the cold, dark water. I can't take in air. But the tidal wave of questions doesn't stop.

What kind of laws could have been passed to stop unarmed kids from getting killed? What will happen to those laws if I save this kid? Will those same laws still exist? Maybe they will but they'll take longer to see the light of day? Is revolution ever piecemeal, or does it have to come all at once?

Let's say I do save this kid and stop him from being murdered—the next Black kid that commits some minor infraction and ends up in the morgue, will that be on me?

"Lala! What's wrong? What's going on?" my dad shouts.

That's when I realize I've been clawing and pulling at my clothes, trying desperately to break free of them and anything else that's touching my skin. I'm sweating and shaking. There's a sharp pain in my chest and my fingers are tingling.

Oh my God, I think I'm dying.

My dad pulls the car over and comes around to the passenger side. "It's okay. You're okay. It's a panic attack. Put your head down."

He rummages in the back seat and finds a crumpled brown paper bag that he places over my mouth.

"Breathe, La, just breathe," he says. He slowly starts counting and tells me to count with him in my head. I do as he says, and *finally*, I begin to regain control of my breathing. I keep the bag over my mouth for a few more labored breaths.

Dad goes to the trunk of the car and brings back a bottle of water. He is always prepared with a supply of bottled water, road flares, and a bunch of other emergency supplies. He hands me the bottle, worry etched on his face. I drink more than half of it without stopping.

"You good?" he asks.

I nod.

"La, what happened? What made you panic? That hasn't happened since your mom."

"I don't know. I think it's just, you know, school and practice. I'm fine now. Really, Dad."

He thinks for a moment, and I know if I don't convince him I'm really okay, we're going to end up in the hospital to have me checked out.

"Dad, I'm one hundred percent better. Can we get home? We're still on the north side. And it's getting late..."

He knows exactly what I mean. He kisses my forehead and gets back in the car. He makes me promise to tell him if I feel another attack coming on. As soon as the car pulls off, a heavy, angry rain starts to pour.

Worst birthday ever.

When we get home, Dad fusses over me and asks if I want to go back to therapy, like I did the first few months after Mom died. I assure him once again that it was just a freak thing and that nothing is wrong with me.

I run to take a shower, wanting to wash the day off me as soon as possible. I then put on my favorite *Rick and Morty* nightshirt, the one that's comfier than a cloud, and join my family in the kitchen.

Dad tells Aunt J and Arlo what happened in the car. Arlo accuses me of trying to get attention. He makes a joke out of it, but I can tell he's relieved I'm okay. Just before the birthday dinner starts, Arlo pulls me aside and into the kitchen.

"It was a Flash, wasn't it?" he asks.

"Yeah."

"Was it about any of us? Are we safe?" he asks.

"It had nothing to do with anyone in this family. And it's probably better you don't know," I say gently.

"La, I know Grandma calls it a gift, but sometimes..."

"Yeah, I know."

Grandma!

I totally forgot with all the drama that happened in the car. I rush into the dining room, where Aunt J and my dad are setting the table.

Aunt J asks how I'm feeling. "I'm okay, thanks. So, um...I forgot to tell you guys something," I begin.

Arlo enters holding two large bowls: one with wild rice and the other with green beans. He places the food on the table.

"Tell us what?" Aunt J says.

"Grandma's coming."

That's it. I didn't know how else to put it, so I just said it outright.

"What? Why?" Dad says. Aunt J gives him a hard look. He softens both his expression and his tone. "I mean, what brings her here so unexpectedly? Is everything okay?"

"Yes. She misses us and wanted to come at the last minute, to celebrate our birthday," I reply as the rain outside shouts louder as if to drown out my lies.

"When is she coming?" Dad asks.

The doorbell rings. I look at the door and then back at my family. "Um...now."

Grandma Sadie has never looked her age. She always looks much younger. And today is no different. She has on her signature crisp white head wrap. She's wearing a flowing flower-print dress. And, as usual, she's adorned with silver ankh bracelets and rings. Grandma and I have the same complexion and the same eyes. Sometimes when I see her, it feels like my mom is staring back at me.

The first person to greet her is Arlo. That's his way of telling Grandma he missed her more than I did and that, in short, he's a better grandchild. He's doing that because he wants her coveted New Orleans pecan pie recipe. Grandma says she's gonna be buried with it. Arlo refuses to give up. And so any time Grandma is here, it gives him yet another chance to try to get the recipe out of her. The two of them can talk for hours about food and the origins of different family recipes.

"Look at you, little boy! You all kinds of grown now, huh?" she says.

"That's right. Note the bass in my voice," Arlo says, purposely lowering his register.

She laughs. "Boy, you a fool, and I love you!" She hugs him again.

"My turn!" Aunt J shouts. The two of them often speak on the phone. Aunt J consults her about her love life all the time. "You didn't tell me you were coming."

"Hell, *I* didn't know, until I knew!" Grandma says.

"Yeah, I know that's right," Aunt J replies with a big smile as they embrace.

Grandma looks over at me with a mix of sympathy and pride. "There's my baby."

"I'm fifteen now, so..."

"So nothing! Come on, give some!" she says. I reach out and hug her. It feels so good to be held by her. She smells like a warm summer night and honey-lemon iced tea.

The last person to greet Grandma Sadie is Dad. His movements are stiff and awkward, to say the least. It's easy to tell by the look on his face that he'd rather be anywhere else right now. They embrace each other like they're each hugging a cactus.

"Hello, Sadie."

"Earl. How have you been?" she asks.

"Fine. Everything here is just fine," Dad says defensively.

"Humph, is it?" she replies.

"Yes, everything is fine."

"Grandma, come try this salmon!" Arlo says as he takes her hand and leads her into the dining room. Dad takes her rolling suitcase and parks it in the corner. He takes a deep breath as if to brace himself.

We all gather at the dinner table, and for the next hour or so, everyone eats and catches up. Dad and Grandma hardly say a word to each other. When we're done with the meal, Arlo and I cut into the triple-chocolate cake that Aunt J picked up for us after work.

Once dinner is over, Dad sends me and Arlo away so he can talk to Grandma. Aunt J leaves to make up the bed for Grandma to sleep in. I still don't know what the issue is with her and Dad. They never give a straight answer when we ask. But now might be a good time to find out. I sneak out of my room and stand outside the dining room, where I hear Dad and Grandma talking.

Though I can't see them, it's hard not to picture the scene: Dad with his elbows on the table, his hands clasped in front of him, covering his mouth. That's the gesture he makes when he's afraid he's going to say something that might be better left unsaid. Grandma Sadie methodically pouring water into the clear teapot and adding loose tea leaves to the cylinder.

"Do you need milk or sugar?" she asks.

"What I need is to know what brings you here, Sadie," he says in a measured tone.

"I missed my grandchildren."

"They've had other birthdays—why didn't you come then?"

"I talk to them often and they come to see me in the summer. I'm in their lives sure as if I was living here, too," she says.

"So, you're here solely because it's the twins' birthday?" he asks.

"Yes—mostly. There has been some development with La's gift..."

Dad laughs sardonically. "Of course! Why else would you be here? That's all you've ever cared about."

"Flashing has been with our family for generations. It's an important tradition, and I won't apologize for caring about it," she replies.

"Is Flashing more important than your own child?" Dad asks.

"What do you want from me? Tell me what I can do to make you stop seeing me as the enemy. I know it still hurts you that Mercy's gone. I'm hurting, too. She was my child. You're not the only one who lost her."

"Don't you dare sit there and act like you were mother of the year," he says bitterly.

She replies angrily, "I warned Mercy not to mess with her gift!"

"She didn't need your warning—she needed your forgiveness! But you couldn't give her that."

"I eventually came to terms with what she did," Grandma replies.

"That's not the same as forgiving her," Dad counters.

"Earl, you know how hardheaded Mercy could be. Once she made up her mind to try and get her gift back, there was no changing it."

Dad groans in frustration. "Do you know why Mercy still sought out healers and mystics all those years later?"

"Yes, she wanted her power back."

Dad shakes his head in disbelief. "No, Sadie. She wanted her mother back. You never looked at Mercy the same way after she lost her gift. You have no idea how much that hurt her."

"I didn't come to argue with you, Earl. I came because Lala needs my help to focus and explore her gift."

"Well, you can forget about it. Lala's focus is exactly where it needs to be—on music and her schoolwork. No more talk about enhancing her ability."

"You can't stop me from helping my own grandchild!"

Dad's voice is ice-cold. "Sadie, you're my wife's mother, you're always welcome here. That being said, you're not teaching Lala anything where Flashing is concerned. You go against my wishes, and so help me, you'll never see my kids again."

NINE

I HEAR DAD HEADED MY DIRECTION, SO I RUSH OFF and go back to my room. I take out my laptop, not because I'm excited to do my school stuff but because I don't want to think about Grandma and my mom's relationship anymore. Also, because I know Dad isn't playing about the deadline he gave me. I have to send in the work I was missing by midnight. I've made the mistake of missing his deadlines before, and he knocked on my door at one in the morning and made me get up to do the work.

He says everyone in the house has a job, and Arlo and I are full-time employees at High School Inc. That's his bad dad joke, letting us know we are not allowed to slack off.

When I'm finished, I email my work to both my teacher and Dad. I'm almost certain I made mistakes, but given everything that's going on, I think I did pretty well.

Rue texts to check on me. She also shares that she's been stress-eating since she got home. I tell her that things are fine and that I'm not freaked out anymore. None of that is true, but what's the sense in making her worry? I don't even tell her about my panic attack because it would just make her stress out more. And Rue deserves some peace, especially after having to hang out with her grandmother yesterday. Argh! That woman is awful.

I know my grandma isn't going to give up teaching me how to expand my vision, so we can figure out where the shooting is going to happen, no matter what Dad says. I text her even though she's just a few yards away in Aunt J's room. I ask what the plan is, and she simply writes, *Do as you normally would, baby.*

Sometimes when I have an awful day, I sneak downstairs and play Grace even though I've already reached the allotted playing limit. If I play for more than that, my body begins to hurt. But right now, I don't care. Today was the absolute worst day, and the only thing that will make me feel like myself is Grace.

I look at the time; it's just after nine. The rain hasn't let up, and it's gotten colder since this afternoon. I grab a sweater to take with me to the basement.

The house is dark. I hear Arlo snoring. Dad's in his room on the phone; I hear him in a low whisper, softly laughing. He must be talking to Candace. I shake my head. I don't have the mental space for the Dad and Candace situation. I don't think they will last; none of us do. The moment Candace admitted she's only seriously dated Black men, we all knew. So why is he holding on?

I guess he's still not ready to face it. I can't judge him for that. I'm not ready to face my grandmother and admit to her that I have not decided what to do about my Flash. She assumes that she convinced me, and, well, she did—in a way. But I still just don't see me standing by and doing nothing when a boy might die.

Okay, enough thinking, Lala. Grace!

In the basement, I turn on the light and close the door behind me. She is standing in the corner. My salvation.

"Hello, beautiful," I greet my cello.

Dad asked if I wanted to decorate the basement so it didn't feel like a dark, hollow room. But that's just the way I like it. We upgraded the lights so I could read the music, but other than that, the space is all but empty. I love it like this, because I can fill it with whatever adventures Grace and I go on.

It takes me almost no time at all to tune Grace. I do a few finger warm-ups so my muscles are nice and relaxed. And then Grace and I take off...

I look at my cell. I've been playing Grace for over an hour. It didn't feel that long. I think that's because I'm finally starting to get the hang of the last measure, the one that's been giving me trouble for the past few days. I hear someone at the basement door. Grandma enters with an African-print tote bag.

"Did you get a Flash that I would be down here?" I ask.

"I know you well enough to know how you handle stress—you go see Grace. I'm sorry your birthday has been so stressful."

"It's one I won't forget," I admit. Then I ask, "Grandma, what's the deal with you and Dad? Why all the arguing?"

She waves me off. "Girl, you know that's grown folks' business, like I said. Don't you worry about it. Both me and your dad are hardheaded, but we still family. That's what matters. Okay?"

No, it's not okay. I would like some answers, but I also

know I need to choose my battles. And this cannot be one of them right now.

She begins to take items out from her tote bag: a large cloth for us to sit on, a box she says contains small vials of essential oils. She spreads some candles throughout the room, then she turns off the light.

"Grandma, it looks like we're about to do yoga."

"We are. But that's just the beginning. Yoga is a good way to begin to let your walls down. Once you are breathing deeply, relaxed, and centered, your mind will be more than ready to do what we need it to do."

"And what's that?" I ask.

"Open up and take you back to the gold Flash," she answers as she spreads out the cloth on the floor. She sits in the lotus position and signals for me to join her.

All those times Rue forced me to do yoga with her during our sleepovers were not in vain. We sit across from each other, and the candlelight reflects off Grandma's face, giving her a warm orange glow.

"It may take a few attempts, but you might be able to access the Flash and zoom in and out of it, like I can with mine. It took years to be able to do that, and we don't have that kind of time, but it's worth a try. Maybe you can pick up small details you didn't get before," she says.

"Did you help my mom learn how to do that?" I ask.

"Mercy wasn't interested in *small* ways to improve her Flash," Grandma replies. "Now, let's begin."

"I think we should talk before we start," I offer.

"Let me say this first. Because of this moment that's about to happen, Black folks can rest at night knowing there will finally be justice for shooting our children in the back like they were dogs on the street. And we're not talking about the kind of justice that only happens north of the Mason-Dixon! There will be a national reckoning.

"I'm grateful the good Lord didn't call me home yet and saw fit to let me be here to witness a new dawn. All because you have the courage to let that Flash play out. I know it won't be easy. That's why I'm so proud of you."

Okay, here we go...

"Grandma—"

"It's getting late, Lala. We need to get started. You have school tomorrow."

"But... Okay."

She starts by asking me to close my eyes and take deep, cleansing breaths. I do as she says, and together we both stay still and just breathe. That's easy. But then she asks me to clear my mind, and, well, that part isn't as easy. When I do yoga with Rue, I can usually clear my mind by playing nice, relaxing music in my head. It's only a matter of time before the notes fill my mind and everything else falls away.

None of that is happening right now. In fact, I'm thinking about literally everything. I think about the gold Flash, school, the three boys, Grace, Aunt J, Dad, Arlo—just about everyone and everything has rented a room in my head. This happens for almost twenty minutes until, eventually, I get frustrated.

"This isn't working!"

"You have to give it time. It takes a while to think about nothing. There's so much going on right now. Don't be hard on yourself. Now, again, deep breath and close your eyes."

I suddenly stop thinking about all the drama and problems I have. But random things that make no sense at all replace them: a rabbit I had when I was six, a pretty pattern I saw on some girl's skirt on TikTok, and gum. That's it, just gum!

"*Argh!*"

"Okay, okay. I can see you're struggling. How about you get some sleep and we will try again tomorrow?" Grandma says as she gets up. She turns the light back on, and we blow out the candles.

"I'm sorry."

"Lala, the first day you held a cello, how did it go?" she asks.

"Badly."

"Yes, because although you loved the sound it made, the cello was new to you. You are new to all of this. It was never going to happen in one day. But I'm here for as long as you need me. Now, get to bed so your dad doesn't kill me."

"Okay, but I want to tell you something..." I reply.

I wish I could play Grace again, because she would give me that boost of confidence I had earlier.

"I get what this movement means, really, I do. And I understand that you want it to happen. I want that, too. So do my dad, Aunt J—just about all the Black folks we know. But that doesn't change the fact that this kid—whoever he is—will have to give his life for this cause. I don't know where I stand with that. I'm not saying I'll change the Flash. I'm saying...I haven't made my decision yet."

"What? Lala—"

"I know how you feel, Grandma, I do. But in the end, I have to do what I think is the right thing, just like Eloise and Lena. Yes, my ancestors sought advice from others, but in the end, they made their own choices. That's all I'm asking, Grandma—for space to make my own choice."

"La, this is way too important—"

"You trust this power, right? Whatever power gave us this gift. So now you have to trust that the gold Flash came to the person it was supposed to," I argue.

Grandma has tears in her eyes. My chest tightens. *Damn.* I'm a horrible grandchild.

I try my best to get her to understand where I'm coming from. I tell her my plan to spend time with each of the three guys. She tells me the same thing that Rue did—it's a mistake to get to know these people. But I push back, letting her know that I feel responsible, and it's only right that I get to know them.

"You won't be doing anything but making it worse. One of them won't be around much longer—why put yourself through that?" she asks.

I reach out and place my hand on her shoulder. "Grandma, I love you. And I'll take all the advice you have to give me. I'll listen closely. But in the end, the decision, good or bad, will be mine."

TEN

THE MORNING RUSH AT MY HOUSE LOOKS LIKE IT does on any other day, except for the addition of Grandma. My brother makes a joke about me being bad at cooking. Dad reminds us of the chores we have yet to do. Aunt J is scrolling through her Facebook feed, hyped about the fact that the number of counterprotesters has grown. But although everything looks the same, it's not. I feel like I'm watching my life from the outside.

I have just six days to make my decision. I was hoping last night would be a success and that I'd be able to nail down the location of the Flash and who the boy is. But since that didn't happen, I hope that Grandma is still willing to help me try again.

She makes us a big pot of buttery grits with shrimp. It's not our usual breakfast, but no one at the table is complaining 'cause it's so good. I have yet to try them, and something in my stomach tells me to keep it that way. I stick with dry toast and cranberry juice. I see Grandma from the corner of my eye, studying me. I think she's trying to gauge if I have made up my mind or not. But I'm not going to decide anything until I've spent some time with the three guys.

"Dad, all this week I have to interview some kids in my school for a report I'm doing about the Confederate flag and clubs like Black Alliance. I have to hang out with them and get a feel for what the club is really like," I announce.

"What class is this for? I didn't see anything like that on any of your upcoming assignments," Dad says.

Argh! Why does he have to be so vigilant about schoolwork? I mean, just this once, can't he be chill about something and just say, "Sure, honey"?

"It's extra credit for World History," I lie. "So can you drop me off after school and come pick me up later, please?" I ask with my best smile.

I can see from the look on his face that Dad's about to ask a million questions. I brace myself, but luckily, Aunt J comes to the rescue. She asks where my interview today is, and I tell her the address that Wes sent to me yesterday.

"I have some supplies I need to pick up for the shop, so I can drop you off. But your dad is gonna need to pick you up."

Dad nods and tells me to call him when I'm ready. "Also, I meant to tell you kids yesterday—Candace is having a gallery opening for an exhibit and invited us all to come. It's Saturday at noon," he says.

We all look at one another, and let's just say not all of us are excited about that prospect—least of all Aunt J. Grandma immediately says she has a lot to do. I'm not sure what she means, but I'm certain it has something to do with my Flash.

"Dad—"

"Arlo, I don't want to hear it. We're going. I know you don't like stuff like that, but it doesn't hurt to explore things outside of your comfort zone."

"Humph," Aunt J mutters.

Dad turns to Grandma and compliments her cooking. And then he ever so gently asks what I'm guessing has been on his mind since she got here: "So, Sadie, how long do we have you here for?"

"I'm not sure yet. But I'll let you know," she replies sweetly. Dad looks like he's doing his best not to roll his eyes at her.

"What the hell?" Aunt J says. We all turn to her; she's scowling as she scrolls on her phone.

"What's wrong?" Arlo says.

Aunt J turns her cell horizontally, so we can get a wide view of the video that someone posted. "It's the camera feed from the Millwood Manor building." We watch two figures wearing ski masks pull up in a dark van. They get out of the vehicle, dragging a black, life-size dummy with them. They wrap a rope around its neck and hang it from the GRAND OPENING SOON sign.

The room falls silent. The air in the kitchen is suddenly thick and difficult to take in. I feel goose bumps down my arms and back, causing me to actually shiver. Arlo looks at Dad as if he can answer all the questions he has in his head. Dad can't. No one can.

We've officially become the town that visitors are warned to stay away from if they happen to be Black. We're the town you ride through and pray to God you never need to stop in. But what happens if that town is your home?

Grandma is the first to recover. She tells us we have school and we need to get going. I know she's trying to put on a brave face. We know this rattles her, too, because her hands are shaking as she stirs the remaining grits in the pot. The next person to speak is Aunt J, but I can't repeat most of what she said without getting grounded.

Dad checks his social media and lets us know that there was another dummy found in the same position—at the home of the president of the group who bought the building. Dad shows it to us reluctantly. He knows it's only a matter of time before we'll find it ourselves.

Aunt J goes off on a rant. She vows that this will only make the counterprotesters work harder to make sure the building opens in six days. She starts calling around, making plans to go to the north side and take her anger with her. None of us can eat anymore. We just say and do normal "get ready" stuff, all the while asking ourselves, *Is this for real?*

"Now go on, y'all, get moving," Grandma says.

"I know the address you're going to after school is on our side, but I still want you to be careful. Do not hang around outside. When you're waiting for me to come get you, wait inside. Got it, La?" Dad asks.

I simply nod.

"And, Arlo, it's straight home for you for a while. I mean it. No hanging out after school with your friends, at least for now. Do I make myself clear?" Dad demands.

He nods.

"Janice..." he says tersely.

"I won't do anything crazy," Aunt J replies. My dad is not convinced and gives her a hard look. "Earl, I mean it." She nods toward him. Dad lowers his shoulders slightly.

"Sadie, please don't leave the house without telling us where you're going," he tells Grandma. "If you need a car, you can use my old one. The keys are by the door. The GPS is a little odd, but it still runs pretty well."

"Thank you, Earl."

"Okay, move it! We have work to do and school to attend," Dad declares.

As we shuffle out of the kitchen, Grandma pulls me aside and lets me know she wants to try again to tap into my Flash after everyone goes to bed.

"Thanks, Grandma."

She grabs my wrist lightly. "I have faith in you. I know you'll do what's right and not what's easy."

When I get to school, the videos are all anyone can talk about. It seems like everyone saw the different clips and has an opinion.

Sand in my locs. Always some speck of sand, no matter how small, finds its way into my head. I will never get it off me. I'll always feel it; it's always there, just below the surface.

Rue runs to embrace me. She won't stop hugging me until I vow that I'm actually okay. And then she asks for a detailed update. She isn't surprised that I can't quiet my mind and get inside the Flash.

"I told you to devote more time to yoga. No one listens," she says as she searches high and low in her locker for her German textbook. She's always losing that thing.

"I know, I'll try again later tonight," I assure her.

"Do you still think hanging out with Wes is a good idea?"

"Maybe it's not, but it's the least I can do. Wish me luck." We don't have a lot of time before the bell rings, but I'm curious, so I ask Rue, "Did you see the videos?"

"Yeah, I saw a few of them," she says. "My parents got into a huge fight because my dad is like, *Let's just leave*, but my mom is determined to stay."

"I'm pretty sure we don't have the money to move. And even if we did, I don't think my dad is ever gonna be good with leaving the home he shared with my mom."

"I saw some of the comments people posted on the videos. It's so odd to be so hated by people you never met," she says, mostly to herself.

"Rue, don't read that stuff. It just messes with your head."

She laughs sardonically. "If you really want your head to be messed with, take a look at some of the people on this thread—some of them are right here at this school."

I look at her cell, and yes, there are some names I recognize, because they have some ego-driven usernames that they mix in with the instrument they play. Some even put a hashtag with the name of our school; that way we know they are not only out there, but *in here*, too.

"Do you *want* to move away?" I ask Rue.

"Our family business started here. This is where I was born. It feels like home."

"I understand, but you didn't answer my question: Do you want to move out of Davey?"

She thinks about it carefully. "My dad has been saying he wants to put bulletproof windows on the town car that picks me up. He's been saying that for years, and my mom and I always talk him out of it. We tell him he's being extra and overprotective.

"We watched both videos this morning and Dad said the same thing he always does about the bulletproof windows. He waited for pushback. He didn't get any."

ELEVEN

WHEN THE SCHOOL DAY IS OVER, I HAVE JUST enough time to sneak in one solid hour of practice before I have to meet up with Wes at his house. We could have done the interview in school, but I wanted to get a glimpse into his life. Again, it's the least I can do for someone I might be sentencing to such a cruel fate.

When Aunt J picks me up, we head to Wes's. I tell her about how Rue's family is considering installing bulletproof windows. My aunt thinks they should have already done that. Sometimes, Aunt J is extra. But this might not be one of the times.

Aunt J tells me there are rumors that Faith & Honor is

planning a march throughout the north side, in full uniform. I'm not sure if that means old-school white hoods and robes, or if they've modernized their outfits. All I know is that nothing good will come from them marching. Aunt J says she's going to a community meeting to discuss what their response should be if Faith & Honor does show up.

"You know Dad is gonna flip if you get any more involved in this. I'm worried about you, too. The protests have already gotten out of hand."

"Well, your dad doesn't run me. I'm grown," she says.

I fold my arms over my chest and give her the side-eye.

"Don't give me that look; you know we need to stand up to these hateful morons. If we don't try to stop them now..." she continues.

I scoff. "You're right. We should do whatever we can to stop them, otherwise this town might become racist," I reply, my voice dripping with sarcasm.

"I know this town is already pretty bad, but we're supposed to be getting better, not worse."

"Just please be careful. I mean, if something happens to you, who's gonna do my hair?"

She laughs and swats my arm.

We pull up to Wes's place and he waves at us from the porch. His house is a single-family home painted bright yellow with cream-colored trim. I get out of the car and wave goodbye to my aunt.

"Are you okay if we talk in the garden out back?" he asks. "My mom's sleeping. She's a nurse and she's been working nights lately, so I try not to wake her."

I nod and follow him around the house. He examines my face and says, "Is it the videos that have you looking so... serious?"

"They don't help," I admit. "Did you read what some of the people posted, some of them from our school?"

My reaction apparently amuses him. "You're surprised?" he asks.

I sigh. "No, not surprised—just over it. My aunt said the Faith and Honor people are planning to march. Did you hear anything about that?" I ask.

"Yeah, Zora and I were talking about it a few days ago. She predicted that they might show up. And not just the ones who live nearby; she thinks it'll be bigger than that with members from neighboring cities joining in."

I'm picking up on something but I'm not sure what. I play a hunch. "So... you and Zora?" And right away, Wes starts to ramble about how it's not a good idea to date someone from the same club. But he can't hide the grin that he flashed once I said Zora's name.

"Wes, you can tell me. I won't spread it around."

"I don't know. She's cool or whatever," he says like an awkward eighth grader. It's so cute. But I'm guessing he doesn't want to hear that. He quickly changes the subject. "Let's get started," he says.

We make our way to the back of the house. I look around the garden. They have planted snap peas, lima beans, and mustard greens. I tell him how much I like it and how much it reminds me of my grandma's garden in New Orleans.

I sit on the steps a few feet away while he gets a bucket full of gardening tools and starts working. He tells me I can ask away whenever I'm ready. I set up my mini tripod and camera and point it at him.

"I'm not really into dirt like that, but I can try to help if you want," I offer.

"Nah, I got it. What do you want to know?"

I learn a fair amount with the first four questions. He joined Black Alliance because he could remember very clearly the first time he was in school and someone called him the N-word.

"Did the kid get in trouble?" I ask.

"Yeah, but I think he thought it was worth it. The minute he said it, the word stuck to me."

"Yeah, I get that," I reply, recalling the time the judge wouldn't shake my hand at the Monroe Competition. I could feel her rejection latch on to me and become some kind of invisible tattoo that only I could see and feel.

I go on to ask him about the Confederate flag being taken down. He says he thinks the flag should be considered the shame of the state and not its pride. When I ask him if the turmoil that comes with trying to change things is worth it, his reply is short and certain: yes. Always.

"So, you're okay with sacrifice if it's in service to the cause?"

"Yeah, I give up two afternoons a week to Black Alliance—that's time away from practicing, but it's worth it to me."

I wonder if he would say the same thing if he knew...

"Okay, only two more questions. First, what is something people would be surprised to know about you?"

"I don't mind elevator music."

"Seriously?"

"I know. I know." He groans.

I stand up, clear my throat, and announce the last question: "This sounds kind of corny, but I'd still like to know: Where do you see yourself in ten years?"

He gets this giddy look on his face and playfully rolls his eyes.

"I know! You're headlining at major concert venues all over the world. I completely get that. I'm gonna start in New York and work my way around the globe," I say.

He laughs. "Wow, that sounds really good. But...not for me."

I'm taken aback by his reply. "Oh, okay. What, then?"

"I'm gonna be a music therapist," he says.

"I've never really thought about music therapy. Why'd you pick that field?"

"My little brother Paul has ASD."

"What's that?"

"Autism spectrum disorder. It used to be called just autism."

"Oh, I'm sorry. I didn't know that," I reply, ready to crawl into a hole. I'm thinking now might be a good time to shut up before I say something ignorant without meaning to.

I guess he can read the hesitation on my face. "La, it's okay to ask questions. Promise."

"Okay...did music therapy help Paul's ASD?"

"When he was around five, things got really bad for a while. He had tantrums all the time, and he was always anxious and on edge. His doctors suggested that my mom try a music therapist. I don't think she believed anything would happen, and hell, neither did I, but we were willing to try.

"We walked into the therapist's office, and she played a song for Paul. 'Row, Row, Row Your Boat.' He listened to the song and started to settle down a little. The more sessions he had, the more positive the outcome. Lala, it was so dope! He just didn't have the right tools to communicate with us. But now, thanks to music, he does. His therapist would let him use different instruments to express feelings of anger, joy, and just about everything in between. We'd implement the same things at home. And eventually instead of shouting or throwing things, he'd play a major chord on the keyboard my mom got him, to show he's happy, or a minor chord if he's not."

"Wow, that's amazing."

"I know, right? I looked into it, and music therapy can help with other things besides ASD: developmental delays, depression, trauma... So many things. I think at first my mom was reluctant to tell people that he was in therapy—you know how we are about that stuff."

"Yeah, I know," I reply. I can recall countless times I've heard Black people say therapy is for rich white folks. But my dad is cool with it and made Arlo and I go see someone when Mom died.

"But now, my mom's okay with it. And she talks up music therapy every chance she gets," he adds.

"So, you're going into the mental health field. I would have never guessed that."

He studies me closely and then says, "What do you call your cello?"

"Grace."

"Okay, remember the first time you played Grace and got through an entire piece of music without any mistakes?"

I sigh as I recall that heavenly day. Wes watches the happy look on my face and says, "Exactly! That feeling you got—when I'm a therapist, I want to use music to give that same feeling to my clients."

"Okay, fine. You win! Your career is a million times more altruistic than mine. Are you happy?" I tease.

He laughs. "It's not a competition, but...yeah, if it were, I'd win!"

"Yeah, yeah," I reply, rolling my eyes. "So, how's your brother doing now?"

"He's good. You wanna meet him?"

"Ah...is that okay?"

"C'mon, let's go!" he says, holding the door open for me. I grab my camera and tripod; we walk through the cozy, tidy house and enter the kitchen.

Paul looks ten, maybe eleven years old. He's sitting at the table, and his blue-framed glasses come complete with matching blue straps. He's in the middle of putting together an impressive and complex puzzle of some Greek goddess of some kind.

Paul looks up occasionally to compare how his puzzle

looks with what's on the box. That's when I get a good look at him. There's no denying he's a cute kid. I call out to him softly, "Hi, Paul."

Paul doesn't look up or acknowledge that I spoke.

Wes whispers, "It can take a little time for him to reply. You can say hello again."

"It's nice to meet you, Paul. I'm Lala."

Paul looks up, says my name, and then giggles.

"I think he likes your name," Wes says. "It might be the fact it repeats. He likes repetition. And also, your name is very musical."

"I like your name, too, Paul."

"Paul, say hello to Lala," Wes tells his little brother.

Paul waves at me, but his eyes don't stay on me too long—they roam about the room and then go back to his project.

Wes says, "He tends to avoid eye contact. He's not trying to be rude—it's just something he does."

"That's okay. I love your puzzle, Paul! How long have you been working on it?" I ask.

Paul consults the digital watch on his wrist and, after a long beat, replies, "Two weeks, three days, ten hours, five minutes, and four seconds...five seconds...six seconds..." He continues to count softly to himself as he dives back into his work.

Wes explains, "We got him a collection of puzzles of Greek mythology. He's really into that stuff. What's the name of this puzzle?" he asks Paul.

Paul doesn't take his eyes away from the puzzle; he simply points to the box, where the title is readily displayed. *The Tragedy of Cassandra of Troy.*

A small series of beeps comes from Paul's watch. "Snack time!" he says, getting up from the table and heading to the fridge.

"Wes, I can go if you need to help," I offer.

"Nah, he does that stuff by himself. He doesn't need me. In fact, he makes all the snacks around here. That's the deal, right, Paul?"

"Right!" Paul says, gathering the ingredients.

"What are you two having?" I ask.

Paul says, "It's Wednesday. Wednesday is yogurt parfait."

We watch him confidently take two prepared glass jars of yogurt from the fridge. He places one down for him and one for his brother. He methodically sets out two small plastic bowls and places a different fruit into each. He gathers the spoons, napkins, and two glasses of water. Everything is meticulously aligned. Paul surveys his work and nods to himself.

"Thank you," Wes says.

It's obvious the brothers have an easy rapport that

shows how much they care about each other. I can't help but feel like I'm intruding.

"Hey, my cell died. Can I use your phone to call my dad and have him pick me up?" I ask.

A pretty woman with the same eyes as Wes enters the kitchen. It's clear from the creases on her face that she just got up.

"Mom, this is my friend, Lala. Can you give her a ride?" Wes asks.

"It's okay," I reply. "I can call my dad."

"It's not a problem, Lala. Let your Dad know I'll be taking you home. I'll get my keys," Ms. Reed replies.

I send my dad a text using Wes's phone and say goodbye to Paul, who waves back. I can't help but smile. He looks so content. And there's no missing the pride in Wes's face when he looks at his little brother.

"Okay, I'm ready—let's go," Ms. Reed calls out.

"Thank you for the interview, Wes. I really appreciate it."

I walk out of the kitchen and feel a knot in my stomach. I try to ignore it as I get into Ms. Reed's car.

"You guys are a really nice family," I say, mostly to myself. And yet another knot makes its way into my belly.

Ms. Reed thinks about it for a second and says, "Yeah, I have good boys…"

"Can I ask you a question, Ms. Reed?"

"Sure, honey."

"Is it hard to raise a child who has ASD alone?"

"I don't know the answer to that question because I've never been alone. I have Wesley. His dad left soon after we discovered Paul had ASD. Too much for him to handle. Paul was three and Wes was eight.

"I didn't know a thing about ASD. I tried to hold it together as best I could. And one day, I was in the kitchen making a pitcher of lemonade. And then, suddenly, I just started sobbing uncontrollably.

"I sat at the table and just broke down. Wes came into the kitchen and made me a promise: He was going to take care of us. And ever since that day, it's been Wesley helping me hold it all together. He pushed me to reach out to other parents in the ASD community, he watches Paul when I work nights, and he makes sure that Paul knows we love and appreciate him just the way he is.

"I was so relieved when he told me he wants to go to college nearby. I would have let him go across the country if that's what he wanted to do. But I'm glad he's staying close. I don't know what we'd do without him."

A lump the size of a golf ball forms in my throat. I turn away from Ms. Reed so she won't see the tears springing to my eyes.

Rue was right—this was a very bad idea...

TWELVE

THE FIRST THING I WANT TO DO WHEN I ENTER the house is run to Grace. I just want to play for as long as possible. It's really the only way I can stop thinking about Wes and his family. But as much as I want to play my cello for hours on end, I know that I need to get my homework done or face Dad.

When it's time for dinner, we all sit at the table and go over our days. I skip the part where I have to decide some poor guy's fate and just go with the standard details: the pieces I'm working on at school and a few other random things.

I can see Grandma Sadie looking at me intently, no doubt wondering what happened when I met with Wes.

As soon as dinner is over, Grandma follows me to my room and confronts me.

"Did you speak to any of the boys?" she asks.

"Yeah, I hung out with Wes today," I reply.

"And?" she says impatiently.

I know how important this is to her and to everyone. But I'm not sure what she wants me to say. How exactly is this conversation supposed to go?

Well, I hung out with Wes. He's a nice enough guy but, yeah, I'm cool with his death quickly approaching.

"Wes is a really nice guy, and he has a family that depends on him," I say out loud.

"I'm sure they do. But you know this isn't about just one family. It's about thousands of families. That's why you should stop this thing you're doing. Getting to know the other two boys is only going to make it that much harder to let things take their natural course."

"Well, the course is wrong! He shouldn't have to give up his life!" I reply, a little louder than I intended. "I'm going to meet up with the other two guys. I'm sorry, but it's what I feel I have to do. But I promise I will let you know as soon as I make up my mind," I reassure her.

She sighs deeply and bites her lower lip like she's trying to keep herself from saying what she really would like to say. She waits a beat and then whispers, "If this is really what you want, I can't stop you. But remember this isn't just about one person."

It's all I can do not to roll my eyes at her. First of all, Grandma would surely snatch them right from their sockets; she's old-school and does not play. And second, I know she's not wrong. There are a lot of lives that will be affected by this. I just wish she'd stop trying to impress upon me how important this is and trust that I get it.

"Are we still on for later tonight?" I ask.

Grandma nods and assures me that we are all set to try again when everyone goes to sleep.

When I finally get to be alone with Grace, it's a welcome break from the drama. She looks lonely. She knows I've been away for way too long. I pick her up and look her over. Just knowing I am about to play already makes me feel better. I start in on one of my favorite pieces: *Adagio in G Minor* by Albinoni. It's a beginner piece that I could play in my sleep, but it's also a calming melody that always puts my mind at ease.

Ever since I received the gold Flash, everything has been a question mark. And now that I'm here in this basement, with Grace in my hands, everything is better. I get so lost in playing that I don't hear Dad until he's right behind me.

"It's late. You need to get some sleep," he says.

"Yeah, I lost track of time."

"As usual. C'mon, upstairs," he says. I put Grace back where she belongs and walk upstairs.

"Everything okay with you and your grandma?" he asks.

"Yeah, everything's fine," I lie. I really hate to do that, but there's no way around it. If Dad knew the decision that had to be made, he'd do everything to try to get me out of it. And I suspect there's no way out.

"Dad, what do you do when all your options are bad ones?"

"That sounds like an ominous question, La. Is everything okay?" he asks.

"Yes, I was just wondering. I have to pick out a piece for a class presentation, and I don't like any we have to choose from."

"There has to be one that appeals to you more than the others," he says.

"Nope, all really bad."

"Well, this may not be about your choice of music. This could be about how you face the challenge of playing something you don't like. Find a way to play the music the best you can, better than you thought you could. Good piece of music or not, you're a professional. Rise to the challenge."

I smile to myself. "Why are you always so sure I can do things?"

"Because you're just like your mama. And when she set her mind on something, she just dove in and got it done. Hell or high water," he replies.

I say good night to Dad. All I have to do is wait for everyone to go to sleep and then meet Grandma in the basement. But while I wait, the memories of my mom that I try to bury come bubbling to the surface.

I recall the first night after we got back from New Orleans, when I had found out about Flashing. My mom came to my room and sat on the edge of my bed. I look at my bed now, and in my mind's eye, she's right there, an arm's reach away.

She said, "You got your first Flash. That's...good." There was a quick expression that appeared on her face. I could have sworn it was resentment. I asked how she lost her gift, and she said it was grown-up stuff and she didn't want to talk about it. I tried to plead, but she said it was time for bed.

"Mom, aren't you gonna tuck me in?" I asked.

"You're grown enough to Flash, I'm sure you can tuck yourself in." Her words were harsh. I don't think she meant for it to come out like that. She softened her tone and added, "You're a big girl now. Go ahead, I'll watch you."

I got myself under the covers. We usually read together, but this time Mom just said good night and turned off the lights. I remember lying there in the dark, tears in my eyes, as my heart sank. I felt like I was in trouble with Mom somehow, but I couldn't figure out what I had done wrong.

My cell dings and pulls me out of my thoughts of the past. It's Grandma, texting me that everyone is fast asleep and I should meet her in the basement. When I open my door, there's stillness in the hallway. The kind that only comes when the household is settled and asleep.

When I get down to the basement, Grandma has everything set up like last time: a large cloth for us to sit on, essential oils and candles throughout the room. We get started. I try to clear my mind, but just like before, the harder I try, the harder it gets. Meditation seems so easy on YouTube. You just close your eyes, and then— *bam!* Enlightenment.

But I guess that's not the way it works in real life, because instead of focusing on the Flash, I find my mind straying back to my mom and grandma again. I remember an argument that the two of them had. I'd blocked it out before but now I can see it play out, like it happened yesterday. Grandma had thought we'd come to New Orleans to share the holidays with her. She was wrong. As soon as we got settled, my mom announced she had an appointment with another mystic. Grandma flipped out.

"Why do you keep going to these snake oil salesmen? It's been years and nothing you've done has brought your gift back," Grandma snaps. She catches herself, takes a deep breath, and tries again. "Mercy, honey, maybe it's time to let this go."

"I can't! I have to try any and everything to get my power back."

"Argh! For the last time, stop thinking of it as a power. That's how you got into all this mess in the first place. It is a gift that was given to our family."

"That's exactly why I have to try and get it back," Mom replies.

"You're just wasting money paying all these scammers," Grandma insists.

"No, I'm not. Her name is Zarita. She is a renowned mystic. She's had a loyal following for years in the bayou."

"If she was the real thing, she'd tell you the truth: There's no way to get back something like that. It's a spiritual, mystical gift that was in our family for generations. It's not something you can send back to Amazon for a replacement if it breaks."

"I can't just give up on this," Mom says.

"Mercy, it's been eight years, let it go!"

Mom laughs sardonically. "Of course, it's easy for you to say, you still have your abilities. You and Lala and every other woman in this family. How do you think that makes me feel, to know that I lost mine?"

"Well, maybe it's for the best," Grandma mutters.

"What does that mean?" Mom demands, folding her arms over her chest.

"Oh, for goodness' sake, Mercy. Wake up! You didn't lose your gift. You threw it away. And now it's gone. Maybe it's time to accept it."

Tears spring to Mom's eyes as she shakes her head angrily. "You're never going to forgive me, are you? I made one mistake, and now you're gonna hold it against me for the rest of my life?!"

"Lala! Are you paying attention?" Grandma says in a loud whisper, jolting me back to the room.

"Oh yeah. Sorry," I reply. "I guess I'm having a really hard time concentrating."

"Try harder. You can do this, La. Now take nice, slow deep breaths," she instructs.

I try to stay focused; I really do. But while my body is doing what Grandma tells it to do, my mind is drifting back to the last time I saw my mom.

She had managed to get an appointment with yet another "highly sought-after" spiritualist, who said she was familiar with the gift and could help replicate it. My mom was beside herself. The lady was only going to be in town for one more night. So my mom was going to see her, even though there was a big storm looming.

Dad begged her not to go because the storm looked like it was going to be bad. It did no good—she was going anyway.

"Can I play Grace?" I ask her as she heads out.

"Yes, but set a timer. You know how you get lost in the music," she says. And then she blows us a kiss and says, "I'll be back before you know it..."

THIRTEEN

NEEDLESS TO SAY, I WASN'T ABLE TO RESURRECT my Flash last night in the basement with Grandma. I just couldn't get my mind to settle. Anytime I focus on having this gift, I always go back to how much my mom wanted it. And once I start down that rabbit hole, there's no space for anything else in my brain.

I remind myself that, like it or not, I have to find a way to clear my head of all the drama and chaos. It's not just about entering my Flash. It's Thursday, and I'm supposed to meet up with Ford. He deserves my undivided attention. If this is his last week on Earth, the least I can do is be present when we're hanging out today.

I just hope Ford doesn't have any adorable siblings, like Wes did. That was just unfair.

"You look so deep in thought. You've been looking that way more and more lately. I would say ever since Grandma came," Dad says, pulling me back inside the car for our morning commute.

"Just school stuff. Rehearsal. No big deal," I reply, keeping my eyes forward.

"You know you can tell me anything—even if I get upset at first, I'm always going to calm down and be there for you. Both you and Arlo."

"Yeah, Dad, I know," I reply. In the corner of my eye I can see his forehead crease with worry. I decide to talk about Candace. I know he wants us to like her, so bringing her up will make him feel better. "So, how's Candace?" I ask in a forced upbeat tone.

He nods, and I watch the tension seep from his shoulders. "She's fine. She asked about you and Arlo and suggested we could do another dinner sometime."

"Sounds okay, I guess."

I don't hate Candace, and I don't mind having dinner with them. The only thing I worry about is just how deeply Dad is falling for her.

"We were thinking a few weeks from now, we might

go away together." He casts his eye on me to gauge how I feel about it.

I do my best to sound positive. "That's nice. Can I throw a wild party while you two are away?" I tease.

He chuckles. "Yeah, sure. But after that party, be sure to let me know what song you want played at your funeral."

"You're gonna be tempted to go with something classic, like Schubert's 'Ave Maria' or Bach, 'Air on the G String.' Fight that urge, Dad."

"Oh really? Okay. And what song will be playing?"

I shrug. "Anything from Nicki Minaj."

"Very classy, La."

A huge man on a motorcycle pulls alongside us, waiting for the light to turn green. He's wearing a leather jacket with over a dozen patches sewn onto its sleeves. I can't see the detail in all of them, but I can make out the two biggest. One is the "okay" sign. I know that sign means "white power" because we had to do a paper on the insurrection that happened a few years ago on January 6. The other patch says FAITH & HONOR in big block letters.

The motorcycle guy is not alone. I look one lane over and there are three other guys, on motorcycles, also wearing leather jackets and patches that let us know what their stance is on people like us. The guy next to us looks inside our car. He gives us a hard stare and curls his lip in disgust.

"Dad..."

Dad puts his hand on my knee. "It's fine, baby. Just relax. We're almost there."

The light changes, and the guy on the bike takes an additional beat to stare us down yet again. The car behind him starts to honk. He finally speeds ahead.

I guess Aunt J, Zora, and Wes were right—the Faith & Honor people really are planning to gather and march. A wave of unease hits me.

I wonder what else they're planning...

The only parts of the school day I remember are the ones where I'm playing Grace (my school cello is also called Grace). And, of course, I remember talking to Ruby. She offered to come with me to meet up with Ford, but I knew she had a private vocal lesson and how much she hated to miss those. So I thanked her but told her I was fine to go alone.

Aunt J picks me up right after school. We follow the directions Ford gave me on the phone. We thought it was for Ford's house, but when we get there, it's not a home—it's a community center. The building is one level and painted light blue with gray trim. There's a sign on top of the building, SUNNY DAYS LEARNING CENTER.

Aunt J tells me she'll wait to make sure I'm in the right place before she drives off. I get out and walk toward the woman sitting at the entrance reading a novel called *Appointment in Samarra*. I ask if it's a good read.

She replies, "Yeah, a little sad, though." She puts her book down. "How can I help you?"

I tell her who I'm looking for and she assures me I'm in the right place and that Ford Stokes is one of the volunteers here. I wave goodbye to Aunt J. The woman at the door asks me to sign in and then directs me to the classroom at the end of the hall.

"You one of them little high school girls that be following Ford around?" she says before going back to her book.

"Um, no. I'm here to interview him about some school stuff. We both go to Ross Academy of Music," I reply.

"Oh yeah? I didn't think that school had anyone that looked like us besides Ford. How many of you is there?" she asks.

"Six."

"Hell, that's five more than I thought. Well, good for you, girl. He right down the hall."

And with that, she returns to her book. I follow her directions and enter a classroom full of what I'm pretty sure are second graders.

The kids are buzzing with activity. Some of them play

with art supplies on their desks, and some are building structures from large, colorful blocks. There's a third cluster of kids in the corner of the room. They sit in a circle and watch as Ford tinkers with a keyboard. He plays a major chord for them. After he plays it, he asks them if the chord was a "happy" chord or a "sad" chord. He signals that he will be right with me.

I nod and look around the room. There's artwork on the wall, done by the kids; posters with tiny kittens "hanging in there"; and a small bookcase with an impressive collection of fables and fairy tales. I walk over to shelve the one book that's been left out of place. I'm about to open it and take a look when Ford comes up to me.

"Hey! Sorry to bring you here, but it was the only time I could fit you in. I have practice the rest of the week," he explains.

"It's all good. How long have you been volunteering here?" I ask.

"Since eighth grade. So, three years. There's usually an after-school teacher that I help out, but she wasn't feeling well, so she went home early."

"She left you here with the kids?"

"Why wouldn't she? I'm good with kids, and I'm responsible. I'm not just a musical genius with a pretty face. I'm layered, Lala," he says with pride.

"And you're humble," I tease.

"Very," he says, dismissing the sarcasm in my voice.

Ford turns to the room and says, "All right, everyone, clean up your area. It's quiet reading time now. Come pick out your books, please." The kids groan but kick into high gear, helping tidy the space and picking up after themselves.

A little boy with jet-black hair and dark eyes comes up to Ford and says something in Spanish. Ford replies to him in the same language. I didn't know he could speak Spanish, let alone was fluent in it. The boy says something in Spanish to his friends, and they all giggle and walk away.

"What did the kid say?" I ask.

"Oh, Jonathan? He told his friends that you must be my new girlfriend."

"The lady at the front desk thought that we had something going on, too."

"I was seeing this girl, and she used to come and hang out with the kids for a while. Now they think any girl I talk to is my girlfriend."

"And you're not seeing her anymore?"

"Why? Interested?" he says with a suggestive smile.

"No. Just curious."

"Nah. I had to break it off. We were hanging out once,

and I told her I had to go or I'd be late for practice, and she actually said, 'Why don't you skip practice?'"

"Skip practice? Yeah, she had to go," I reply.

"Exactly. Okay, we have a few minutes—what do you need to know?" He takes me to the teacher's desk, where two chairs are waiting. We each take a seat, and he angles his chair so that he can see all the kids. I take out my camera and aim it at him—while he's answering questions, he never once takes his eyes off the kids.

I have to admit, there's more to Ford than I originally thought. When I ask him about why he joined Black Alliance, he tells me it's because he comes from a long history of activists. His grandfather was a Black Panther, his dad organized a series of protests in college, and his mom is an active member of the NAACP. So getting involved is very much a family thing.

When it comes to the Confederate flag, his reason is different from Wes's. Ford wants the flag taken down because he considers it a beacon to white supremacists everywhere. He feels that the flag tells them that here in this town, we welcome hate.

"So for you, the flag is basically a calling card to hate groups, like a siren song calls out to sailors?" I ask.

"Yeah, I guess that's a good way to put it. If I were in

a hate group, that's a symbol I would look for if I were looking for a place to live. We can't let Davey continue to be that place."

"You know about the drama going on about diversifying the north side. There's been protests, fighting, and all-out chaos. Looking at that, do you think all the turmoil is worth it? Is it ever too much trouble to take a stand? I won't judge," I assure him.

"There's only one of me. I can't stand up for every single issue. But when I find an issue that 'sticks to my ribs,' like my grandfather used to say, I'm gonna go hard for it. No matter what."

"And the flag is your issue?" I ask.

"Yes. That flag should have been taken down long ago. And I'm here to help make that happen in any way I can."

The conviction in his eyes is undeniable. I rarely see him being this serious and impassioned about anything that doesn't have to do with girls.

"Second to last question: Ford, what would people be surprised to know about you?"

"I don't just wake up like this. It takes good hair products, a vigorous workout, and relentless adherence to my skin-care routine."

I look up at him, thinking he's joking, but he's not. He is, in fact, very serious.

"Did you charm your parents into paying for your private piano lessons?" I ask.

"My parents have better jobs now, but when I first got into music, we had no money for lessons," he confides.

"Yeah, I get it. There was a point where I think my dad was working ten jobs," I joke. "So, how'd they end up paying for private lessons?"

He tells the kids that they can come up and pick which musical instruments they want to try out for the day. They squeal with excitement and go over to the large blue bin full of small musical instruments, ranging from a xylophone to a tambourine.

"Paying for lessons wasn't possible for us back then. We were living in Mississippi. I was about seven. There was this old lady in our neighborhood. She used to look outside her window every day and report whatever bad things we did to our parents. Her name was Ms. Cord. But we used to call her Ms. Crow. She was a retired music teacher. And sometimes she'd give private lessons in her house."

"Did she give you lessons at a huge discount?"

He shakes his head. "Nah, what she gave me was one good pop on my behind. It didn't hurt, but from an old lady, it had a little sting to it."

I can't help but laugh at the picture in my head of a

young Ford getting smacked on his butt by a mean old lady. "What did you do to get hit?" I ask.

"We were throwing pebbles at her window in the middle of one of her lessons. Everyone got away but me. After she popped me, she made me stand in the corner and called my parents."

"What did they say?" I ask.

"She could keep me as long as she wanted and make me do chores for her! The betrayal was deep."

"I've never met your parents, but I think I love them," I reply with a smirk.

"Yeah, yeah. Anyway, she was giving a piano lesson to a girl who kept messing up. I got annoyed, and I was like, 'Don't you hear the next note? Why do you keep missing it?'

"And the crow was like, 'Fine, you're so smart, you play!' And I did. I played by ear and repeated it perfectly.

"She said I had an ear for music and joked that I might not be useless after all. But I didn't want to play. I said classical music was 'white people music.' She made me watch documentaries about William Grant Still, Herbie Hancock, and Nina Simone. It became our thing. We'd watch the greats and talk about their style, technique, and interpretation. She taught me for years and never asked for a dime."

"Is she still around?"

"No. She got sick just before I auditioned to get into our school. They thought she'd only live another three to four months, but she lived much longer than that. That old crow refused to die until she found out if I got into the school.

"The week I got my acceptance letter, I showed it to her. She got all choked up and said, 'Now, don't go into that school acting a damn fool, hear?' But I think that was her way of saying she was proud of me. After she died, we learned that she supported a lot of other kids who couldn't afford lessons. That's where most of her retirement money went."

"I'm sorry she's gone," I reply awkwardly.

"All good. I know she's looking down on me every day, judging my posture as I play. And I swear I can still hear that woman's voice, calling out for me, when my lesson is about to start: 'Boy, you best get yo' ashy self over here and learn this piece.'"

He takes out his cell and shows me a picture of his mentor. She was a stout, dark-skinned woman with full lips and a salt-and-pepper Afro.

"She looks like such a badass!" I mutter.

"Yeah, she was..." he replies, sinking deeper and deeper into the picture. I can almost feel how much he's missing her by the way he studies her face. I know how easily I can fall into sadness when it comes to remembering my mom, so I try to move on and get him back to his usual boastful self.

"All right, one last question: Where do you see yourself in ten years?"

And right away, Ford gives me his trademark boyish grin and says, "Playing in the biggest venues in the world, with a fine honey on my arm—you know how a brotha do!"

Okay, he's back...

"But that'll only be in the summer months. The rest of the year, I'll be teaching and supervising the classical department at the music school."

"What music school?"

"The one my family and I are gonna open in honor of Ms. Cord. The Edna Cord Academy of Music and Arts. And my fame in the classical world will get us the investors we need to open the school. We're gonna teach hip-hop, funk, jazz, and classical. No more separation, you know? I want our students to know that there's no such thing as 'white music.' And that music is universal; they have a right to any and all forms of it."

He gets super excited and starts talking a mile a minute about how his school's sole focus will be on making classical music more accessible to kids who can't afford lessons. He's got everything so well laid out, it's as if the school is already built.

"I know I get carried away. But opening a school is something I've wanted to do forever. I can't wait! Lala, it's gonna change this town!" he promises.

An adorable little girl with two pigtails and red-framed glasses tugs on Ford's shirt. "Mr. Ford, Marcus won't let me take a turn on the drums!"

"Okay, Tiana, I'll be right there," he says. I can't get over how relaxed and at ease he is with the crowd of kids. He looks like he's already a teacher.

"I better go and handle this. Marcus doesn't know what he's in for—Tiana's a biter!" he says.

I tug my lower lip to keep from smiling. "You better hurry."

He starts to walk away but then turns around to face me one last time. "Is it stupid?" he asks in another rare serious moment.

"What?"

"Opening a school here? Do you think I can do it?" he asks.

"No doubt."

He grins. "Sometimes, I worry that it won't happen. But it will. It might take a few more years than I thought, but still, no big deal. I got all the time in the world, right?" He chuckles and turns his attention to the kids.

I rush out of the room and close the door behind me. I put my hand over my mouth as tears run down my face.

"*I got all the time in the world, right?*"

FOURTEEN

FRIDAY AFTERNOON IS BRIGHT AND CRISP AS Aunt J's car pulls up to the bowling alley. I look over my outfit. Last night, after yet another failed session with Grandma, I called Rue. After I filled her in on my time with Ford, we went over what I should wear to meet Alex. In the end, we settled on a dark blue hoodie dress with ankle boots and hoop earrings. I think I look pretty good, but I could still use a confidence boost.

I stay in my seat, too nervous to leave the car yet. I guess Aunt J can read my mind, because she turns to me and says, "La, that outfit is too cute to waste on just me. Go!"

"I really look okay?" I ask.

"Girl, you look good enough to make your dad nervous about ever letting you out the house."

I beam and thank her for both the compliment and the ride. I jump out of the car and enter the Lucky Lanes bowling alley.

The place is alive with neon lights, loud music, and the cacophony that comes with a room full of teenagers and crashing bowling pins. I've been here a few times with my family but never saw Alex working here. Again, Alex isn't my one and only thought, but when I do think about him, my heart actually skips a beat.

He's standing in the shoe rental window, handing out shoes to the customers. He's wearing a hideous purple uniform shirt with gold trim. There's a name tag on his uniform with the company logo—a cartoon bowling pin with muscled arms.

How can he still look hot in such an ugly uniform?

He has a long line of customers waiting to get their shoes, so I stand off to the side and wait for him to be done. It's about ten minutes later when the line finally settles down and he waves for me to come inside the shoe rental room.

"Hey, sorry about that—sometimes the lines can get a little nuts," Alex shouts over the roar of the crowd.

I shout back, "It's cool. Are you sure we can talk here, at your job? I don't want to get you in trouble."

"We're good. My boss is out of town, and the assistant manager is really laid-back. Also, I have a break coming, so he's gonna relieve me."

The moment he says that, a guy who looks to be in his early twenties enters the rental room, wearing the same hideous uniform. "You ready for your break, man?" he says.

"Yeah. Um, Lala, this is my assistant manager, Harold." We say a quick hello to each other, and Alex takes me to the back room. Inside there are two seats, a wall of jackets, and a poster promoting Lucky Lanes. The space is small, dimly lit, and about as romantic as going to the dentist. But the fact that it's just us two, in close proximity, makes me a little nervous.

"It might be too loud to—" I don't have to finish my sentence, because as soon as Alex closes the door, the noise from the bowlers is cut down by more than half. Now we can actually hear each other without needing to shout.

From the corner of my eye, I spot something that I missed before—a vase of red flowers sitting on the windowsill. Its petals are long and curve toward the sun.

"What kind of flowers are these? It looks like a spider on its back," I tell him.

"Funny you should say that—it's called a red spider lily. It's also called the resurrection lily. I know because Harold told me that's what the florist called it. His girlfriend has a thing for odd flowers. So, I'm guessing he's gonna give them to her on their date tonight. Here, have a seat," Alex says, his hands shaking slightly as he pulls out my chair for me. I'm not sure why they're shaking—maybe he's nervous about the interview, or maybe he's had too much coffee. I see a bunch of discarded coffee cups in the trash bin next to the desk. Alex sits at the table across from me. I take out my camera and the tripod, and in a few minutes, I'm all set up.

"Is your boss okay with your being in his office?" I ask.

"This is just for the employees. My boss's office is near the front entrance; it's bigger and doesn't look like the perfect space to interrogate someone," he quips.

"You're right. This room does have a good cop/bad cop vibe."

"Sorry, this was the only time I could do the interview. Any other time, I'm in Black Alliance or—"

"Practicing. Got it," I reply. "I didn't know you worked here. I've come a few times with my dad and my brother, Arlo, and we never see you. Did you just start working here?"

"Ah...there may have been a few times when I saw you and your family. And I may have fled to the back."

"What?" I laugh. "Wait, why?"

He looks at me, and at once, it becomes very clear that he likes me, maybe as much as I like him. He fiddles with the stapler in front of him and can't maintain eye contact for more than a few seconds.

"Oh. Okay," I reply, not sure what else to say.

"I'm sorry. I wasn't trying to make this awkward," he says as his voice cracks. Oh, my goodness! I can't stop smiling, but I don't want him to think that I'm having fun at his expense. I'm just kind of thrilled that he might actually like me, too.

"Don't worry about it. It's all good. Maybe next time, you'll come by and say hi," I suggest.

"Okay, maybe I will."

Oh great, now I'm blushing. I clear my throat and pray that the butterflies in my stomach settle down.

We start the interview, and the more we talk, the easier it gets. He tells me that his reason for joining Black Alliance was that he wanted to be a part of a group he could relate to. He talks about how hard it is to be in a school where almost no one looks like him. He says that's why it surprised him that I didn't want to join the club at first.

"Well, it's just that... it's a lot. Everything in Davey is *a lot*," I reply.

He nods with understanding. "Yeah, I can see that. But I'm glad you're gonna be a part of our group now."

"Thanks. So, why should the Confederate flag be taken down?" I ask.

"For the same reasons we would get rid of a Nazi symbol—it's revolting and offensive."

"I get that. We did a whole section on the Holocaust last year. I could actually feel my heart breaking, just reading about all the horrific things that happened."

"My mom took our whole family to the Holocaust Museum in Houston. After that we had planned to go to lunch, but it just seemed wrong to experience that and then go have fries."

I nod. "Yeah, I felt the same way when our family went to an exhibit about the Underground Railroad. That kind of brings me to the next question: The turmoil that comes with trying to make changes in this town—is it worth it?"

"I never ask myself that," he admits.

"Really? Why?"

He shrugs. "It never occurs to me that I have a choice. It's a struggle. But we pick up where the ones before us left off. And when I die, my kids will take up from where I left off. But I'm hoping by that time, there's so little racism, we march for small things."

I quickly jump in. "Like Black hair-care products in

fancy hotel rooms—my aunt is a hairstylist, and shampoos and conditioners that don't treat 4C hair are the bane of her existence."

He laughs. "Well then, that's what we'll march for a few years from now. Do you want a Coke or something?" he asks.

"Sure." I stop the recording. He opens the door, and the noise filters back in. He returns shortly with two cans of Coke and hands me one. We drink quietly and stare at each other. The more eye contact we make, the warmer my face feels. I remind myself that I'm not here to gawk at the guy I like. I have a mission: get to know Alex.

"Next question: What don't people know about you?" I ask.

"Can we come back to that?" he says sheepishly.

"Yeah, sure. Last question: Where do you see yourself in ten years?" I ask.

"Well, violin is basically my whole life. But composing always takes me to a whole new level. So I plan to do more of that. I'm going to do a double major when I get to Juilliard. It's rare that they let you, but I think I can swing it."

I smile at the thought of the two of us going to the same conservatory. "So in ten years, we'll see you composing major pieces all over the world?"

"I've already started to work on something," he says.

"You have?"

"Yeah, it started out as a small passion project and just grew and grew."

I proceed carefully, because not all artists like to share what they are working on at the moment. "You don't have to show it to me, but can you tell me a little more about what you're composing?"

"Do you know August Wilson, the playwright?" he asks.

"Yeah, my dad took us to see one of his plays when it came to Houston."

"He wrote ten plays, each documenting a decade in Black America. Ten plays covering one hundred years. That's what I want to do. I'd like to compose a piece for every decade after the Civil Rights Movement. By the time I'm fifty, I'll be done. Hopefully."

"Fifty!"

He laughs. "I know, right? But it doesn't matter how long it takes; I'm in no hurry to get it all done right now."

Yeah, I know. You have all the time in the world.

He takes out his cell and shows me a video of him tinkering on the piano, playing the first few bars. "The music is coming to me in pieces, and not necessarily in order. It's like unraveling a mystery, one musical phrase at a time."

I hear the start of the melody in my head, and it gives

me chills to think of it being played in full. I think about the subtle tension he's already begun to build in just a few measures. "Alex, this is beautiful..."

"I'm really happy about where it's going," he says, showing the first hint of self-confidence. He smiles at me, and the room starts to spin, in the best way. I close my eyes, take a deep breath, and make the room stay still.

"I can't wait to see how it turns out," I admit.

"Thanks."

"What did everyone else say when you showed it to them?" I ask.

"I haven't. You're the only one who has seen this. It's personal. You can't just share with anyone, right?" He laughs nervously.

"So... why did you show it to me?"

"You're not just anyone. I remember seeing you at the audition to get into our school. I was sitting a few rows behind you. And you held on to your cello for dear life because you were so nervous. You had these big eyes and were trying so hard not to look overwhelmed."

I sigh. "Yeah, I remember. I didn't know you were there that day," I reply.

"I was. And I wanted to come by and wish you luck, but once you opened your cello case, you didn't need any encouragement. You were ready. And you were... brave."

I roll my eyes. "Well, maybe in that moment, but when I got home, I was terrified I wouldn't get in," I confess. "And even after I did get in, I would have nightmares where it was all a big mistake, and I didn't *really* make it in."

"The point is you were brave. Braver than me. There's something I've been trying to do since last year and can't get the nerve to do it—it has to do with your other question: what you don't know about me."

"All right, what don't I know about you?" I ask, intrigued.

"I've been trying to get the nerve to ask you out since last year."

My heart leaps into my throat, and I think there's a good chance it'll stay there forever.

"I picture us on a date all the time but can't get around to asking you. I'm hoping to work up to it."

"I think you just did."

He looks away. "Yeah, I guess I did."

"Where do you see us going on this date in your head?"

"Sometimes the park? A movie. A concert. Doesn't matter. I just like the fact that we're, you know...together."

"Okay, so after this date to an unknown location for an unspecified event, what happens?" I ask.

"What do you mean?"

"How does our date end?"

He gives me a sly but still very shy smile. "Ah...we kiss."

Please, God, don't let it be Alex in my Flash.

"We're in Texas and we're prone to tornados and hurricanes. There's just no telling when the end will come. So, maybe we just skip to the last few moments of our hypothetical date. Maybe you just kiss me now."

WTH?

Did I just say that out loud? I just said that out loud!

"You want me to kiss you?" he says.

I could be coy. I probably should be. But knowing what I know, I'm all out of time for coy. "Yes, I'd like that—but only if you want to," I reply, offering him a way out.

He nods but doesn't speak. His face is a mix of excitement and panic. I have no idea how to work out the mechanics of the situation.

Does he get up and kiss me? Do I get up and go to him? Should we be sitting or standing? Are we going for a friendly peck or a real kiss with tongue? Who goes right and who goes left?

While I'm busy overthinking, he comes around and sits on the edge of the table. He takes my hand and guides me up, so that I am standing before him. He's taller than me, so we're at eye level now.

He leans toward me. The music coming from outside is drowned out by the sound of my heart pounding against my rib cage. If I have a heart attack now, I'm gonna be so mad!

I close my eyes. Our lips touch. He parts mine with his tongue. He tastes like summer and Coca-Cola. We slowly pull apart. I open my eyes and look down. I realize that the whole time we were kissing, he never let go of my hand.

I'm not sure what's supposed to happen next. I don't know anything about post–first kiss etiquette. But I don't need to worry, because he has to get back to work. He walks me out to the lobby, where I can wait for my ride. We say goodbye and exchange shy, content smiles. I wait until he's completely out of sight and call Rue.

I have never heard Rue squeal as high as she does now. There's nothing in her training as a vocalist that could account for such a high pitch. I think it's a special pitch reserved only for fifteen-year-old girls.

"Tell. Me. Everything!" Ruby says.

Rue is never happy with just broad strokes. She wants all the details. What did the air smell like? How long was the kiss? And did we have our eyes open or closed? I do my very best as her BFF and spill all the tea.

"We have to hang out tomorrow. That way you can tell me everything—again," Rue says.

"I just told you everything."

"Nope. It's different in person," she informs me.

"I'm sure you're right, but my dad is making us go to Candace's art gallery tomorrow. She's unveiling some new artist."

"Argh! Does your dad know his love life is getting in the way of our girl time?"

I laugh. "I'll be sure and tell him," I reply.

"Okay—hey, La?"

"Yeah?"

"I'm glad you had your first kiss."

That's when it really hits me: That could've been Alex's *last* kiss. He's fifteen; it shouldn't be his last anything. And that goes for all three of them.

What the heck was I thinking?

I can't let Alex or any of them get hurt, let alone die. I'm sorry about the movement and what it means for us as a whole. But I will not stand by and let this Flash happen. Period.

Tomorrow, when we come back from the gallery, I'll let Grandma know. I realize she won't take it well, and I dread telling her. But it feels good to finally come to a decision. And I think I made the right one.

FIFTEEN

THE CANDACE BECKER ART GALLERY IS LOCATED in the heart of the north side. It's about ten minutes down the road from the Manor, where all the protesting is taking place.

We enter, and the first thing that gets my attention, as always anywhere, is the music playing—Chopin, Nocturne Op. 9 No. 2. It's a little predictable, but I get why Candace picked it. It has the calming, serene effect that an event like this needs.

The gallery is one large room. Although the space itself isn't huge, it's elegant and has a high-end feel thanks to the warm walnut floors and stark white walls. There are a few white benches scattered around so the guests can sit and study the artwork.

The show is all big photographs of different sizes expertly framed and hanging on the walls. All the photos are in black and white and feature close-ups of Black body parts. None of the photos feature faces. The highlight of the exhibit is a large image depicting a dark-skinned Black man's sculptured torso.

There are twenty-five or so people mingling around. Candace is in the center of a group of women, playing host. She's introducing them to a tall, lean man with pale skin, a thin mustache, and a beret.

"Who is that guy?" Aunt J asks.

"I think he's the artist," Dad replies.

"Why is he dressed like a silent movie villain?" Arlo quips.

"He definitely looks like he should be tying some poor woman to the train tracks," I reply.

Dad gives us his patented "behave" look and waves to Candace. When she sees us, she excuses herself and comes over. She gives my dad a kiss. She greets us with the same enthusiasm.

"I'm so glad you all came! I can't wait to hear what everyone thinks," Candace says. "That guy over there is Tim Cross. This is his exhibit. He's a massive talent. Doesn't his work just *move* you?"

"It's...interesting," Dad says, smiling awkwardly.

Candace places her hand on Dad's arm and looks sincerely into his eyes. "Oh, Earl, I hope it was okay to bring the kids. I figure they're already into more sophisticated things than most teens; Arlo is into fine dining and Lala is a cellist, so...I thought they would appreciate this kind of art."

He smiles. "No, it's fine."

Candace teases, "It's definitely a conversation starter. And that's the point of art, right? To start a dialogue."

"No one has faces," Aunt J mutters.

Candace studies her. "Janice, you don't like the art?" she asks, sounding hurt.

Aunt J is about to reply to Candace, but then she catches my dad's eye. And his expression tells her he would not appreciate her honest take on the art.

Aunt J instead says, "I'm just not used to this kind of art, but I'm sure everyone else will like it."

Candace breathes a sigh of relief. "I hope so. We put so much work into this. I can't wait for you to meet Tim. This is all his work. He's the next big thing in the photography world."

Someone in the crowd waves to her. "I have to go, but I'll be back. In the meantime, please, take a look around."

She makes her way toward a small group of women with expensive-looking handbags.

"Let's give this thing a chance, okay? We might see something we like," Dad says.

Aunt J and Arlo scoff at the same time.

"What?" Dad asks.

Arlo shakes his head, bemused. "We're the only Black people here, in a room full of white folks who 'admire' our bodies."

"So?" Dad replies.

"So, we're just gonna act like we're not in the first thirty minutes of *Get Out?*" Arlo says. Aunt J bursts out laughing. I try to suppress a smile, but it's hard.

"This might not be like that. Maybe this artist is trying to highlight the beauty and inner strength of the Black community," Dad says.

"That must be why no one from the Black community is here," Aunt J retorts. Dad flashes her a warning glare. Arlo looks down, attempting to hide his grin.

"Okay, Dad, we'll look around," I say.

"Thank you!" Dad says, still glaring at Aunt J. She sticks her tongue out at him.

I tell both of them, "Hey, don't make me separate you two!"

We walk over to the photo of the torso. There's a bald guy with bushy eyebrows and tinted glasses standing next to us. He nibbles on the end of his glasses thoughtfully and remarks, "Such power; such brute strength..."

We make our way to the photo featuring a toned back and broad shoulders. We hear a man remark to the woman next to him, "Outstanding physique." She nods in agreement.

A few minutes later, a woman with red hair and a pretty green blouse looks at the photo of a muscular thigh and simply says, "Yum." The other ladies around her all laugh.

"All right, we're leaving," Dad says between clenched teeth. He marches us toward the exit.

Candace sees us and hurries over. "You're going already? You just got here. There's a little mixer after this, and there's nonalcoholic stuff for the kids to drink."

"No, thank you. We have to go," Dad says. He's trying to keep his voice level, but the anger behind his tone is making that difficult.

Candace takes Dad's hand and pulls him aside to talk to him. But we are still close enough to hear what's being said. I kind of wish we weren't.

"Earl, honey, what's wrong?" Candace asks.

"Are you really asking me that?"

"Yes."

"You don't see what the problem is?" Dad asks in utter disbelief. "Have you heard anything these people have been saying?"

"Did someone say something wrong to you or the kids? You let me know and I'll throw them out!" she says with conviction.

Dad looks at her, and his anger dies, replaced with exhaustion and resignation. "No, it's not... We're gonna go." He motions for all of us to leave. We walk out; Candace follows.

"Wait!" she shouts. Dad turns to face her. It's clear she wants the two of them to talk alone. It's also clear Dad is not up for that right now. "Earl, I really like what we have," she whispers.

"Me too," he says, mostly to himself.

"Okay, then... Look, I'm not sure what happened today, but we'll talk tomorrow. And you'll explain it to me. I feel like I'm missing something."

"Yeah, you think?" Arlo mumbles. I jab him in the ribs, and he groans.

"Let's talk tomorrow. I'll call you," Dad says, giving her a quick kiss. She waves goodbye and we wave back.

On the way home, we're all pretty quiet. Dad is driving, but he's a million miles away. The only sound comes from the music playing: Stevie Wonder singing "Superstition."

We drive by the Manor, where the number of protesters and counterprotesters continues to grow. I can't remember ever seeing that place without them. There are two cop cars standing by—it seems they, too, have become permanent fixtures.

A new Stevie Wonder song comes on, "My Cherie Amour." Dad's eyes are shiny from unshed tears. He quickly blinks them away, but Arlo and I see him in the rearview mirror.

"Dad, you okay?" my brother asks.

Dad swallows hard and nods. "Yeah. Your mom used to love this song."

All of us look at him as if he's grown horns. Dad never talks about Mom. All the pictures of her in his bedroom are at a certain angle where he can't really get a look without having to reposition them. He can't bring himself to take them away but can't stand to see her face every day, either.

"'My Cherie Amour' was Mom's favorite? I don't remember ever hearing her sing that," I admit.

"I do!" Aunt J says. "Earl, didn't she try to learn French just because of that song?"

Dad replies, "Yes! I'd forgotten about that."

"Mom knew how to speak French?" Arlo asks.

Both Aunt J and Dad laugh.

"She tried, but she was awful," Dad says. "She just couldn't get her tongue around French, or any foreign language, for that matter. But it didn't stop her from trying. Once she got it into her head to try something, she was gonna do it all the way."

He turns up the music. "This is her favorite part coming up. The only French she could ever speak!" he says, laughing at the thought.

We all start singing the chorus at the top of our lungs. I'd like to think Mom's shouting along with us.

When we enter the house, Dad heads straight for the kitchen. I peer inside and watch him sitting at the table. He's drinking a bottle of root beer, drifting off into outer space. His mood is somber. He looks as if he's hoisted the whole world onto his shoulders and is just now feeling the full weight of it. He's too lost in thought to note that I'm there.

"What's up?" Arlo asks.

"Dad's really upset about the gallery," I whisper once he's closer to me.

"Maybe, but he shouldn't be surprised," Arlo says.

"What do we say to him?"

He thinks for a moment and then replies, "I got this. You go to your room."

"What are you gonna do? Don't joke around—this isn't the time for it," I warn.

"Excuse you. I said I got this," he says, affronted. He signals for me to go away and then enters the kitchen.

I get that it's rude to spy, but curiosity gets the better of me. And besides, I'm not sure I trust Arlo to have a sarcasm-free conversation with anyone. I listen to the scene play out and hope he doesn't make it worse.

"Dad, I'm making a sandwich, you want one?" he asks.

Dad jumps slightly at the sound of Arlo's voice. "What? Oh no. I'm good. Thank you."

"You know what, I'm gonna make you one anyway. In case you change your mind."

Dad just nods absentmindedly.

"Dad, can we talk, man to man?" Arlo asks.

Dad suppresses a smile and nods. "Of course."

"When you first told us about Candace, I had an issue with it because I didn't want anyone to replace Mom."

"I get that, Arlo, I really do. And you don't have to try to take it all in at once. Candace and I are going slow. We're not rushing you or your sister. This kind of thing takes time."

"I agree. I'm sure, in time, we'll all be cool with her. But that's not the only issue I have with her."

Dad exhales loudly and nods. "Okay, what's your issue with Candace?"

Arlo keeps working on the sandwich while he remains deep in thought. Dad silently waits and braces himself.

"You remember that white girl I used to hang with back in summer camp a few years ago, Allison?"

"She had braces and curly hair, right?"

"Yeah, that's her," Arlo says. "She had a good comeback for everything, and she understood that video games are an art form. I loved hanging out with her."

"What happened? One day she was coming over all the time and then she just stopped. Did you two have an argument?" Dad asks.

"Allison invited me to dinner at her house. I was excited about getting to meet her family. They made a really good dinner; we ate and told jokes. It was nice. Later that night, as she was walking me out, she confided in me. She told me that her dad loved using the N-word and her mom made it a point to clutch her handbag whenever anyone that looked like me walked by her.

"Allison had been trying hard to get her family to be more tolerant, and getting a Black friend to come to dinner was part of that plan. She was really proud of herself. She got to show off her nonviolent, nonthreatening Black friend. The entire dinner I'd sat there, feeling like I was a guest, but I wasn't—I was an exhibit."

"Why didn't you tell me?" Dad says, concerned.

Arlo shrugs. "There's nothing you could have done, Dad. It was just one of those things. The reason I'm bringing it up is because, well, as far as you and Candace go... I'm not saying you shouldn't date her. I'm just saying be careful. Trust me, you never want to find yourself on display."

SIXTEEN

I'M NOT SURE IF WHAT ARLO TOLD DAD HELPS HIM or makes things worse. All I know is that he's going for a drive, which he never does unless he's got serious things on his mind.

In the meantime, I go to my room to practice how I am going to tell Grandma my decision. But no matter how I try, I can't get the right words together.

I soon give up and go play Grace. And even though I am still messing up on the piece I'm practicing, just holding Grace makes me feel better. It's only when I'm playing that I know exactly what to do and who I am.

Once I'm done, I run up to my room to hide. I'm just too scared to tell Grandma I've made up my mind.

Okay, Lala, stop being a punk and go talk to her!

But instead of going to knock on her door, I find myself in the kitchen.

Coward.

Dad comes back home just before dark. He's on a call. "No, Candace, that's not what I meant." He runs his hands over his head. "Hold on," he says. He enters the kitchen and scours the pantry. He mutes his cell and asks, "What happened to my Funyuns? Did we run out of my Funyuns? I swear I saw a bag here."

Uh-oh. That's Dad's favorite comfort food. I'm guessing the call isn't going well.

"Funyuns? Even if I knew where you could find a bag, I wouldn't tell you. I refuse to aid in your culinary demise," I reply.

Dad's about to say something but, in the end, decides to go back to his call. "You're right. I don't know the art world like you do, and I get that you weren't trying to—" He looks at me, and I guess he's not happy with the fact that I'm just standing there overhearing his conversation.

"You need something, La?" he says, covering the phone with his hand.

"No, just wanted to know if you're okay," I reply.

"Oh, this?" he says. "It's fine. Candace and I are fine," he adds, stitching together what he thinks is a confident smile. He goes into his bedroom and closes the door.

I guess needing comfort food is a family trait, because all I want is my go-to food—Frosted Flakes. I reach into the pantry and take out a brand-new box. I don't bother with milk or a bowl. I open it and dig in. This entire box is for me. I'm claiming it. I sit down at the table and shovel handfuls of sugary deliciousness into my mouth.

"I'm gonna need you to have a little more shame," Arlo says when he enters the kitchen and sees me.

"Go away. I'm busy," I warn him.

"This is your version of busy?" he asks.

I nod. "Yes. I'm busy sublimating my anxiety with sugar."

He sits down across from me. It makes sense; he rarely does what I ask. "Why are you so anxious? Is it Grace? Are you still struggling with that piece you've been working on?"

"I don't have it nailed yet, but that's not it. I have to tell someone something, and I know they'll be really disappointed in me."

"Oh no, did you go back to putting ketchup on your eggs again? I work so hard to refine your palate!"

I shove yet another handful of cereal into my mouth and shake my head.

Arlo thinks for a moment and then says, "Just say it quickly and get it over with. That's what I do."

"Yeah, I know," I reply bitterly. "I remember the time you dropped my favorite doll into the sewer and then ran to my room and said, 'Yo, Sasha's dead. Sorry. Bye!'"

"Yeah, kind of like that," he says. I glare at him, and as I crunch away, he smirks. "I had just watched *It* on TV. And I thought there might have been a clown in the sewer. I had to get something to lure him out. Tying a rope around your doll and lowering her into the grate was good thinking. She was the perfect size. I didn't know she'd slip out of her harness. Blame Stephen King."

I roll my eyes at him and shovel more food into my mouth. Aunt J enters the kitchen and sees me tearing into the bright blue box.

"Damn, it's like that?" she says.

"It is, and no, I don't wanna talk about it," I reply.

"Okay. But I'm here if you need me. Also, there's a new box of Corn Pops in the pantry—that's my dinner. Touch it and it will be your last meal," she warns.

Arlo shakes his head in utter disbelief. "Funyuns? Frosted Flakes? Corn Pops? How do I stop you people from eating like five-year-olds on Halloween?" he asks.

"I might let go of my Corn Pops plans, but only if dinner happens to be jambalaya," she says slyly.

"Fine. I don't have everything I need; I'll have to get some stuff delivered," Arlo says. Aunt J rushes over, gives him a kiss on the cheek, and bounces out of the room. He sighs. "The things I do to keep my family away from a culinary black hole," he says, taking out his cell to place the order on his app.

Gray spirals flash

1812 overture

ushers in

lovers

turned

enemies

misjudge

misgivings

mistrust.

Everything is

black.

And

white.

So, nothing is black and white.

The gray Flash plays out like it's happening right then and there. I see Dad and Candace at the gallery. It's only the two of them, and they're in the middle of a heated discussion.

"*You're holding me responsible for what other people are saying about the art? How is that fair?*" she demands.

Dad shakes his head, incredulous. "*What did you expect, Candace? This wasn't an art show—this was an auction block.*"

"*Is that who you think I am? That I'm some ignorant, out-of-touch white lady who gets off on embarrassing people of color?*"

"*No, of course not,*" he replies.

Candace exhales and takes Dad's hand in hers. She looks him in the eye and speaks with heartbreaking sincerity. "*I disagree with you completely. I think the art was about celebrating its subjects, not demeaning them. But, Earl, I'm not willing to end our relationship on a difference of opinion. I love you.*"

"*I love you, too,*" he admits.

"*Then let go of all the other stuff.*"

Dad scoffs bitterly. "*That's just it—I don't have the luxury of letting go.*"

He studies her. I can practically see him daydreaming about

a life with her. But then his eye lands on one of the photos on the wall. He takes a beat and then addresses Candace.

"Do you ever ask yourself why you only date Black men?"

"It's just my preference," she replies.

"You don't think you have any preconceived notions in your head about us that are driving your decisions?"

"No, I don't," she says.

He groans in frustration. "We can't even start to address this if you're not willing to admit the truth."

"And what truth is that?"

"A part of you is seeking us out because you have some stereotype swirling around in your head about Black men."

Candace reflects and then shakes her head sadly. "This isn't about me. It's about you and your insistence on making everything about race. I'm not like that. I don't narrow my worldview down to race. I love you for you. I don't even see your—"

Candace falls silent.

They both know the rest of the phrase; there was no need for her to finish it. They also know something else: It's over. Maybe even before it ever began...

My mind settles back to the present, where Arlo is about to put his phone away. "Hey, Arlo?"

"Yeah?"

"Add a bag of Funyuns."

He studies me. "I saw you zone out. A Flash?"

I nod.

"Dad and Candace?" he asks.

"Yeah."

"How bad is it?" he says.

I think over the scene and the hurt look on both of their faces. "He's gonna need the party size."

Arlo and I go out of our way to be extra nice to Dad, because even though he doesn't know it yet, sometime soon, he's gonna be heartbroken. Thinking about Dad and Candace gave me a much-needed break from my other anxiety. But now that I'm headed down to the basement to meet with Grandma again, it is back, and in full force.

"Are you ready to start?" Grandma asks.

I can feel tension make its way down my body. My stomach feels like it's on a roller coaster with no safeguards. I know I can't let that stop me from telling her what I need to say. "Grandma, I think we should talk."

"As soon as we are done here."

I'm relieved I get to stall for another hour or so. "Maybe I should try playing Grace. It could help me relax so I can get into the Flash."

"It's worth a try," she says.

Grandma gets the candles, oils, and cloth ready. I hold Grace and close my eyes. The moment I glide my bow across the surface of the cello, I can feel my body begin to relax. I continue to play, and it doesn't take long for me to leave the basement in my mind's eye. I feel light and have no cares at all.

I hear Grandma's voice reminding me to take deep breaths. She tells me to let the music become the soundtrack for the gold Flash. She doesn't need to encourage me—I know right away that this is a world I cannot only control but master. I feel my body get pulled from the basement and thrown inside a tunnel...

I'm standing still, but everything around me is moving at unimaginable speed. Things are going so fast, I can't make out anything other than a blur of light. I continue to play Grace, but I do it dolce; soft and sweet. I hope that will slow down this whirlwind. It works! The wind dies down and gives way to a thick, dense, gold-colored fog.

There's a huge spotlight on all the elements of my Flash—the porch, the white door, and the boy. Everything that's more than three yards away is bathed in darkness on all sides. It's basically a re-creation of my Flash, but on a stage.

The boy stands facing the door. A shadow falls on his face. The more I try to see it, the more darkness hides his features. I stand facing him and wave. But nothing happens. I don't think he sees me. I look over his shoulder, attempting to see what street we're on. There are no discernible signs or markings anywhere. This could be almost any street in Davey.

I turn my attention back to the boy; he's looking around, just like I am. I didn't notice that before. Maybe he's lost. He knocks. The door opens, and the old man's eyes are filled with hate. His mouth is curled into a determined sneer. His knees are slightly bent, and both hands are on his gun. I force myself to focus on his surroundings, desperate to find out something new . . .

I feel someone shaking me. "La, are you okay? You blacked out," Grandma says.

I open my eyes and find her leaning over me. There's worry and uncertainty etched on her face. "I'm fine," I promise her. Once she looks me over and sees that I'm telling the truth, she begins to settle down.

"Did you find out who the boy was?"

"No, but I know where the shooter lives."

I tell her how I looked over the man's shoulder and saw clearly into his foyer. There was a pale green credenza with a vase of flowers and an open envelope—with his address clearly marked.

"That's good, but you didn't see who the boy was?" she asks.

"It doesn't matter. Now that I know where the shooter

lives, I'll be there at the right time and stop Alex, Ford, or Wes from knocking on the door. I'm gonna look up the house."

"Lala!" she says, the strain in her voice undeniable. I look up and find her scowling at me.

"I'm sorry, Grandma, but I'm going to save him—whoever he is."

I enter the address on my cell and see the street view of where the old man lives. And his door matches what I saw in my Flash. He lives only a few miles away, before you are officially on the north side.

She takes a calming breath and says, "I'd like to propose something. You gave the boys your time. You went into their lives and got to know a little about them. I think you should grant me the same consideration. I want to take you to New Orleans tomorrow. There are a few things I want to show you—things you need to see before you make your final decision."

This is an impossible choice, and I don't want to go back on it. Grandma senses that and says, "This is a major decision. You can spare a few hours to make sure you're making the right one."

"What about Dad?" I ask, desperate for a reason not to go.

"I'll take care of it," she says.

"I don't know..." I mutter as my stomach twists itself into knots, each tighter than the last.

"New Orleans is less than two hours away. We'll go and come back same day."

I look at her with a mix of hesitation and exhaustion.

"Lala, I'll say this and then I will leave it up to you: If you are actually certain that saving the boy is what you should do, then nothing I show you tomorrow will change that."

I feel a warm stream of tears run down my face. "I want this to be over," I admit, hanging my head.

"I know, baby," she says, wiping my tears away.

I look up but I don't speak. The lump in my throat makes words difficult to form. I just nod. Looks like I'm headed for New Orleans...

SEVENTEEN

EARLY THE NEXT MORNING, GRANDMA AND I take a taxi to the airport. Her cell dings several times. And soon whomever was texting her moves on to calling. She says it's my dad and answers the call.

So, apparently when Grandma said she'd take care of it, she meant she'd blindside Dad and tell him just moments before we got in the cab. The two of them argue, and I can hear him shouting from the other side of the call. He begrudgingly agrees to let us go, but only because he has no idea we are leaving Texas and because Grandma tells him that if she can spend the day with me, she'll cut her visit short.

We land in New Orleans less than two hours later. Grandma rents a car and drives us to the oldest Black neighborhood in the United States: Tremé.

"What are we doing here?" I ask.

"We're going to see a good friend of mine, Dr. Davis. He's a retired history professor from Howard University. Now works part-time as curator at the New Orleans African American Museum. Nick—Dr. Davis—agreed to give us a quick tour before the doors officially open for the day," she says.

She parks the car in front of a two-story pale blue house with white trim. There are brightly colored murals of historical Black figures painted on the walls outside. The museum looks more like a home than a business. We walk up to the gate, but it's locked. Grandma takes out her cell and sends a text message.

A few minutes later, a man appears on the front porch and makes his way toward us. He's about Grandma's age, with salt-and-pepper hair that's more salt than pepper. He's tall and wears the kind of glasses you'd expect to see on someone who works in a museum.

When he sees us, he beams—more specifically, when he sees Grandma. He takes out a set of keys and unlocks the gate.

"Cookie!" he says as he takes her in.

"It's good to see you, Nick," she says, returning his smile. They share a warm embrace. "This is my granddaughter, Lala."

"Nice to meet you, young lady," he says. We shake hands, and then he turns to Grandma and says, "I see she got your good looks."

"Don't you start now..." Grandma warns with a coy smile.

Wait, is Grandma flirting?

Dr. Davis makes his way inside and tells us to follow. Once his back is turned, I nudge Grandma. "Cookie?" I ask.

"Hush. Get'n in grown folks' business..." she says in a disapproving tone.

"What kind of *business* do you two have?" I tease.

She rolls her eyes, but it's only to distract from her mischievous grin. He tells us he normally doesn't give private showings but that he would do anything for Grandma—or should I say "Cookie."

We follow Dr. Davis inside, where beautiful masterful works of art surround us.

There's a section on the north wall dedicated to the antislavery movement. In the center of that display hangs a portrait of powerhouse abolitionist Harriet Tubman.

It's made up of crumpled WANTED: HARRIET TUBMAN

posters. The artist arranged it so that the papers, when assembled, depict the fearless leader's proud, defiant face.

On the opposite wall hang mixed-media portraits of the three civil rights giants: Dr. Martin Luther King Jr., Rosa Parks, and Malcolm X. Below the paintings is a glass display featuring multiple artifacts associated with their legacies.

There's a banner on the east wall that reads TELLING OUR STORIES, and under that banner is an exhibit illustrating the Middle Passage in a stunningly detailed quilt, using vibrant African prints. "That's gorgeous," I say as I move in closer to examine the stitching.

Grandma says, "Look up, baby." I follow her gaze, and above our heads are wooden sculptures of slaves taking flight. It's a re-creation of the cover of a book Dad read to us all the time when we were kids: *The People Could Fly*. The way the quilt and the sculptures are arranged, it looks as if the figures in the quilt have morphed into airborne figures from the storybook.

"I'd love to give you a full tour, but Cookie tells me you're on a tight schedule. And that I am to focus on the exhibit behind you," Dr. Davis says, pointing to the west wall.

I turn to the direction he's pointing. The wall is adorned with black-and-white photos taken during the Civil Rights

Era. The banner above the photos reads THE FORGOTTEN WOMEN OF BLOODY SUNDAY.

"We switch out the photos depending on the theme for that season. This season, since it's under attack yet again, we decided to highlight the turbulent and tortuous road that led to the Voting Rights Act," Dr. Davis says.

Grandma scowls and says, "Humph." I know all about the new attempts to stop Black people from registering to vote because my dad has launched into more than a few tirades after watching the news. It got to the point where we forbade him from discussing politics at the table. He refused to go along with this new rule, but in a twist of irony, we voted on it and he lost.

"Lala, do you know what led to the Voting Rights Act?" Dr. Davis asks.

I take a deep breath and chew on my lower lip. "I don't remember all the details..." I mutter as my face grows warm with embarrassment. In my defense, I didn't know there would be a quiz.

I do pretty well in my academic classes, but I only hold on to the info long enough to pass the test and get a good grade. Once that's over, all the knowledge I had seeps out of my head. That's fine with me; it allows more room for music.

"Tell us what you do remember," Grandma says.

"Um... okay. To protest all the ways we were prevented from registering to vote, a peaceful march was held in Alabama. There were hundreds of people in attendance. The goal was to walk across some bridge to go from Selma to Montgomery."

"And do you know if they made it across?" Grandma asks.

"I thought they did—didn't they?" I ask.

Grandma says, "Once the protesters got to the bridge, they were met with a mob of state troopers. The governor ordered the troopers to attack the crowd with tear gas and billy clubs. No one died, but a lot of protesters were seriously hurt. And they had to turn back. That day became known as Bloody Sunday. And soon after that, the Voting Rights Act was passed."

Dr. Davis nods. "Days after Bloody Sunday, three additional marches would take place, making way for the Voting Rights Act. The bill made it illegal to put into practice anything that would deny anyone the right to vote based on race."

I look at the larger-than-life photo of protesters getting hit in the head and tear-gassed. The troopers wear malicious expressions on their faces as they beat the crowd into submission.

"All that and they didn't even get across the bridge?

How messed up was that? Argh! Seriously, what is the point? There's always going to be some kind of roadblock preventing us from getting to that elusive 'other side.'"

"Try not to be discouraged," Grandma says.

"She's right," Dr. Davis adds. He draws my attention to the two largest photos on that wall. In one photo, a Black woman is holding a protest sign above her head with a determined look on her face. "The woman in the photo on the right was Viola Jackson. She was taking part in a different peaceful protest where she was chased into a restaurant and beaten."

"Was she able to get away?" I ask.

"Her son came to her defense and was shot and killed by a state trooper for doing so," Dr. Davis replies. "Seeing that happen pushed John Lewis and many others to organize the march that would become Bloody Sunday."

"And what about the other photo?" I ask, pointing to a portrait of a woman who's gone limp and is being held up by fellow protesters.

Grandma says, "That's Amelia Boynton Robinson—she was nearly beaten to death on Bloody Sunday. The photos of her brutal attack made headlines and caused nationwide support for the movement."

"We place Mrs. Jackson and Mrs. Robinson at the center of this exhibit because without them and many other women, there would have never been a Voting Rights Act," Dr. Davis says.

I've seen pictures like these online often, when doing research for school. But there's something different about the pictures now that they are larger than life and I can really see the whites of the women's eyes. It makes me think they are in 3-D and will pop out of the art at any moment.

Dr. Davis looks toward the painting of Dr. King. "People like Dr. King and John Lewis get the credit—and deservedly so—but the fact is that never in all of human history has a movement taken place without the help of ordinary people, taking extraordinary risks."

"I couldn't do it. I'd never be that strong or that courageous," I whisper. "I'd be way too scared."

"Oh, I'm sure they were plenty scared, Lala. But they did what had to be done because the movement was bigger than their fears."

Dr. Davis looks into my eyes, and a smile appears on his face. "Cookie told me you're a gifted cellist. And that classical music is your passion." I nod. "Well, think of it this way, young lady," he says. "Like music, a movement relies heavily on time. These women, like many others, knew the time had come."

EIGHTEEN

OUR NEXT STOP IS THE LOUISIANA BAYOU. THIS place makes no apologies for its heavy heat and ubiquitous fog. Spanish moss drapes lazily off the twisted branches of the bald cypress trees. Croaking frogs, buzzing flies, and tapping woodpeckers provide the background music. Other inhabitants use silence for cover—the lizards crawling on dead trees, the hordes of gnats hovering above our heads, and the worms wiggling in and out of the muddy swamp floor.

The animals that covet silence the most are the alligators. The algae-riddled, murky swamp stands eerily still. And yet I know they are there, just beneath the surface.

Grandma Sadie used to take us to places like this when we came to visit for the summer. She had friends that lived near the swamps, and she'd have them show us around.

I'm not afraid of the bayou, but I'm also not thrilled to be here. When I was little, I believed that places like these held secrets that I didn't want to uncover. It made the hairs on the back of my neck stand up and made me shiver. I still feel like I did back then. And also, there's the matter of the mosquitoes feasting on my arms and legs.

I'd like to rush and get where we are going, but I know the bayou is a place where every step should be taken with care, so I'm more than okay with our snail's pace. We are about twenty minutes deep into the wetlands before we spot a run-down wooden shack house on stilts sticking out of the water.

The house was at one point painted a bright green, but now only a few flaky patches of paint remain. It looks as if a gust of wind could blow it apart with very little effort. Although the structure is the only man-made thing around here, it blends in well with the landscape. It's as if the shack was born out of the swamp.

There's someone perched on a chair in the front of the shack. Their head is down, preventing me from seeing his or her face. All I can make out from where we are is the wide-brimmed, sun-faded straw hat. They are seated with their right leg crossed over their left knee. There's something about the way the person folds into himself or herself that reminds me of a treble clef.

To get to the porch, we gingerly step on a series of mud-soaked planks that serve as a makeshift walkway. If the person hears us approaching, they do not let on. They remain as still as the surface of the grimy water below.

Grandma calls out to the figure as we get closer, "Ça va, Lafayette?" I don't speak Cajun, but I've been around enough of Grandma's friends to pick up a few words and expressions. She just said, "Are you well, Lafayette?"

The figure, who is apparently named Lafayette, does not move until we are standing in front of them. And then the person lifts their head and speaks for the first time. "Ça va, all right," she says.

The woman's skin is so black, she could've walked out of a Kerry James Marshall painting. Her complexion is so absorbing, it's impossible not to be pulled into its orbit. Lafayette is tall and thin. She looks to be in her late seventies, but could easily be older. She stands up; despite her age, there is no frailty in her movement.

"You're late, cher," she says with a thick Cajun accent.

"We came as soon as we could," Grandma says. She then turns her attention toward me. "Lafayette, this is Lala. My granddaughter."

I reach out so we can shake hands, but Lafayette is hesitant. She looks at Grandma for guidance.

"Lafayette's the oldest female in the Boudreaux family. And like us, they were given a gift. Only, while our family can see ahead, the Boudreaux can see the past—anyone's past. Especially if they were to shake that person's hand."

"So, giving her a handshake would be like letting her read my journal?" I ask.

"Oui," Lafayette replies with a mysterious grin.

I don't want her knowing my past. I also don't want to appear rude, either. I retract my hand, but slowly.

She laughs. "I understand. Fifteen is a special age. The age of secrets and discovery. You may hold on to yours."

The three of us walk inside the shack. There's a large room with a small wooden table, three chairs, an old-school stove with just two burners, and a dark hallway. But the thing that I note most is the aromatic scent of Cajun spices that fills my nostrils and makes my mouth water.

I follow the heavenly scent to the burners on the stove. There's a teakettle on one of them. The other burner holds a small cast-iron pot with the lid on.

"What smells so good?" I ask.

Lafayette lifts the pot's lid and shows me the contents. Grandma replies, "Lafayette is known all throughout this area for her alligator sausage gumbo. It's a local treasure."

"Merci, cher," Lafayette says. "I would offer you some, Lala, but sometimes Traveling can make people queasy."

"We're going somewhere?" I ask.

She says yes and then takes a tin cup from the cabinet to the right of the stove. She takes the kettle off the stove and pours its contents into the tin cup.

"This is a special herbal tea my great-grandmother made for us, the ones who had the gift. It soothes the mind and causes the body to enter a soft, sleeplike state. Please, drink," Lafayette says.

I look at Grandma, and she nods that I should drink. I sniff the tin cup; it smells earthy, with a hint of chamomile. "What's in it?" I ask.

"Hops flower, valerian root, and chamomile. In addition to some other items that are a family secret," Lafayette replies.

"Are you drinking, too?" I ask.

"I've had my gift for over seventy years now. I no longer need anything to get my mind and body ready. Please, drink."

I pick up the cup and sip. It tastes like fresh dirt and what I imagine maggots must taste like. I recoil.

Lafayette is amused. "The more you drink, the easier it will be to get to where we need to go."

"And where exactly am I going?"

She replies, "March seventh, 1965. Bloody Sunday."

I feel panic and terror cover me like a weighted blanket. I turn to Grandma, my eyes wide in distress. "No! Please. I can't!"

Grandma takes my hand. "You're not going to the march. You won't see the bridge or any kind of violence, I promise."

"But she said we're going to Bloody Sunday. What else is there but violence?" I demand.

"That's just it, baby. There was more to that day than the ugliness reported on the news. That's where she's taking you to—the morning of the protest, before the bridge. I want you to see the sparks of change that were ignited earlier that day. Lala, as much blood as revolution demands, there is also an uncanny sense of pride and purpose. I want you to witness that firsthand."

Lafayette says, "Try to relax. And remember, all these events have already happened. You can't change them. All you can do is try to understand them."

My eyelids grow heavy and droop. Lafayette takes my hand in hers. "Do not let go of my hand, understand, cher? Do not let go."

I nod, or at least I try to, but my head is too heavy. And now, unable to keep my eyes closed, I give in to the darkness...

When I open my eyes again, the shack is gone. I'm standing on a street corner, and judging by the way the crowd looks past us, they don't know we're there. Lafayette and I watch as they gather. The crowd is mostly Black, with a handful of white people. The ages range from college students to elderly men and women.

The chill in the air does little to dampen the energy of the crowd. They talk among themselves with excitement and fervor. They chatter about which part of town they've come from and the personal reasons that brought them here.

The guy standing a few feet away from me addresses the woman behind him. "After what they did to Jimmie Jackson, no way I was gonna stay home. Nah, I got to be here!"

She replies, "I had my mama watch the kids to come on down here." The certainty in her voice lets everyone around her know she has no regrets about showing up.

There's a group of students, not far from me, wearing TUSKEGEE UNIVERSITY sweatshirts. One of them asks the group what happens when they are victorious and are actually able to vote without fear of retaliation.

A guy among the group with a dark blue fedora replies, "Man, I'm going on down to the voting place with my best suit and my best strut. They ain't even ready!" He demonstrates his walk, taking exaggerated steps. And with each step, his grin gets bigger.

The guy next to him says, "I'm not even gonna walk. I'm gonna do that James Brown slide, right on in." He does his best James Brown imitation, and his friends laugh.

I zoom in on a group of church ladies with big hats and Bibles tucked under their arms. They are in the middle of a prayer and seem to be only moments from getting the Holy Ghost.

I catch bits and pieces of conversation from parents who came so their kids will one day be able to vote without fear. I overhear the tail end of a conversation between two old men where one of them tells the other that if this is the last thing he does on this Earth, it will have been worth it.

The longer we stand there, the more people join and the louder the crowd becomes. The exhilaration and sense of duty is palpable. It's as if they all agreed years before to meet here on this day, at this time, and fix what was once thought of as unfixable.

Someone in the crowd begins to hum a hymn I don't know. I watch as others in the crowd join in. Their resilience and boundless optimism gives me chills. It feels more like a massive family reunion than a crowd of strangers. And although they lead different lives, they are all bound up in this one moment.

The leaders of the march are too far away for me to see, but I guess they've given the order to begin, because the crowd starts walking forward. Their steps are purposeful and resolute. For the crowd of protesters, there simply is no turning back.

I want to be near them. I want to feel their limitless hope and resolve. I didn't realize, until this moment, just how lacking I am in both, at least when it comes to the race stuff. I run. I run from Black Alliance, the counterprotest going on in front of the Manor, and I'm running full speed ahead to get out of Davey. I'm always running. I need to ask them how it is they found unshakable faith when it has long eluded me.

I step forward to follow, because I don't want to lose the warmth and hopefulness they bring to me. Lafayette shakes her head. "They are headed for the bridge. We cannot follow."

The street goes dark. My eyes are once again heavy. I give in and close them.

When I open them again, I'm back in the shack, in the bayou.

I tell Grandma she was right—I did get a whole new look at that era and what it meant to be there. I got to see and feel the energy that came with the start of a movement, the start of national change.

I don't tell her that I was gutted as I stood still and watched the crowd go past me. I don't mention wanting to follow along and be a part of it. I can't say it out loud, but I feel the loss of that warmth the crowd gave to me. The farther away they got, the colder I felt inside.

NINETEEN

THE LAST STOP ON GRANDMA'S TOUR TAKES US to Lafourche Parish. She pulls off the main road and turns onto a long, winding path with giant bald cypress trees on either side. Up ahead stands a striking two-story plantation home with a white balcony, tall columns, and a wraparound porch.

"Where are we?" I ask as she pulls up in front of the house and turns off the engine.

She keeps her eyes forward, takes a deep breath, and swallows hard, but says nothing. I ask her again, and she replies, but never looks me in the eye. "This place is called Oak View. But more importantly, this is a Jump house."

"What's a Jump house?"

Before she can reply, the front door opens and a group of Black kids bursts through. There are seven of them, ranging from about six to twelve years old. They're talking and laughing among themselves. I can't really make out what they are saying, but they seem excited about something.

The boy in the front, wearing a red cap, waves to us. Grandma and I wave back. And while the other kids behind him run around to the backyard, the kid in the hat comes toward us. I follow Grandma out of the car.

"Auntie Lou said we were gonna have guests. Is that you?" he asks.

"Yes," Grandma says with a somber smile.

"Hi! I'm Matthew—not Matt. I don't like the name Matt," he warns us.

I can't help but smile at the certainty in his voice. I'm guessing people often shorten his name.

Grandma nods. "All right, Matthew. You can call me Ms. Sadie, and this is my granddaughter, Lala."

I nod and smile at Matthew. He looks me over, and his suspicion grows. "Someone named you Lala? That's weird."

"Yeah, it is a little. But I'm used to it now," I reply, trying to suppress a smile.

"Auntie Lou says when you come to someone's house,

you supposed to bring something. Did you bring us anything?" he asks, folding his arms across his chest.

"Sorry, next time," Grandma replies.

The front door opens again, and an imposing woman with microbeads piled high atop her head appears. She's wearing a crisp white dress. She puts one hand on her hip and gives Matthew a keen stare.

"Little boy, go on and play. Stop bothering folks," she orders him.

Matthew rolls his eyes, although he's careful not to let the woman at the door see him. "See you later," he says before taking off in the same direction as the other kids.

Grandma introduces me to the lady, whose name is Luenell. She greets me with a smile and kind eyes. "You can call me Lou; everyone does. Come on in."

Once inside, I note the beauty of her home. The high vaulted ceilings, the hardwood floors, and the grand staircase. There's something else that captures my attention—the steady stream of kids running around.

There are two girls, a little older than me, sitting on the steps of the staircase. They're wearing clothes that are straight out of the '80s. I'm sure they're exchanging juicy gossip with each other. I know that look well. The other kids that zoom by us are mostly too involved with each other to look our way.

Lou guides us to the kitchen. It smells wonderful, reminding me of citrus and warm summers. And as if reading my mind, Lou says, "That scent is from my simmer pot. I just throw in some lemon peels, orange rind, and cinnamon sticks. Makes the house smell nice."

We sit at the table, and Lou's in the middle of serving us some sweet tea when we hear loud thumping from heavy footsteps outside the kitchen.

"I don't know what all y'all doing out there that you need to be so loud," Lou yells.

"We just goin' up the stairs," a little kid says.

"Well, stomping ain't gonna get you there any faster!" she shouts back, never once taking her eyes off the tea she's pouring.

"Sorry, Auntie Lou," a different voice replies.

She shakes her head as if irritated, but there's a small smile she tries to suppress. I think she likes the chaos. "Them kids love working my last nerve, I tell you."

A guy about my age enters the kitchen. He's wearing a red Kangol bucket hat, a thick, twisted gold chain, and a colorful Troop jacket. He looks like he's from a different era.

"Auntie Lou, me and Sonya wanna go down by the pond," he says.

"Manners, Donald," she scolds him.

Donald turns to us and says, "Oh, my bad. Hi."

We greet him, and he looks back toward Lou for her final decision. "Go ahead, but take some of them noisy kids with you," she says. Donald agrees and takes off.

I look out the kitchen window; it faces the back of the house. The kids we saw earlier are climbing a huge tree, racing to see which one of them can get higher. The ones in the race are determined to keep climbing, and the kids on the ground are cheering them on. But soon they have climbed too high, causing my heart to skip.

"Lou, I think someone's gonna fall out of the tree. They should get down," I tell her.

Grandma and Lou exchange a cryptic look as the kids climb higher. "Don't worry, they'll be just fine," Lou replies.

I look at Grandma, and she, too, isn't the least bit concerned about the heights that the kids are reaching.

"How many kids are here?" I ask.

"The number goes up and down. It can be as little as twenty or as big as seventy-five. It really depends," Lou says.

"What is this place?" I ask.

"This is a Jump house," Lou informs me.

"That's what Grandma called it back in the car. I'm sorry, I don't know what that means," I admit.

Lou looks over at my grandma, who nods slightly.

"When you die, you go into the light. There are many different words for that, but we call it Jumping. And as you know, there are many ways that a person's life can end: old age, car accidents, heart attacks, etc. When that happens, they simply Jump, and their souls will be at peace. However, for children whose death came about directly or indirectly because of their skin color, the soul can't Jump into the light. They cannot find the peace they deserve."

Grandma sees the look of confusion on my face and spells it out for me: "Lala, this is a house that holds the souls of dead children who cannot move on until justice has been done. They're stuck here."

Lou looks sadly out the window as she watches Matthew climb to the highest branch. She speaks in a small, faraway voice. "They just linger here, and the longer they stay, the more decayed their spirits get."

"No," I object, standing up. "You're telling me those kids out there are, what—ghosts?"

"Yes," Grandma replies.

My heart is racing now, and I can feel beads of sweat on my forehead. I feel a cold chill run down my body.

Lou comes toward me and takes my hand in hers. "Abigail gave your family the gift to see a small piece of what is to come. My family was given a gift, too—we can access the veil between the dead and the living. We can see the souls of those who can't Jump and are trapped here. I think she did that to ensure there would be someone to look after them." She walks me to the window. "Look out there, what do you see?" she asks.

"If that's your family's gift, how is it that we can see them, too?" I ask.

"You can see them because I'm allowing you to. I could lower the veil and you'd think we're in an empty house that rattles and is still 'settling,'" Lou replies.

I'm so shaken, I'm not sure I can form a sentence. And so I just shrug. She asks me again what I see. "I see some happy, healthy kids playing."

Lou opens the window and calls out to them, "Y'all go on and play by the pond with the older kids." The children do as she says and steer away from the house.

She tells me to keep looking at them as they walk to the clearing in the backwoods. I watch, dumbfounded, as the kids' appearances change completely. Their skins are bluish-gray and hang off their skeletal frames. Their faces are hollowed out and their eyes are devoid of life.

There are two of them with small holes in their backs: Matthew and another boy. There's a girl with the same hole, except it's on her right side. The last two hold their heads at an odd angle. Like they're paused in the middle of getting their necks broken.

"Why do they look like that?" I ask.

"All the souls are either assigned to a Jump house or gravitate there due to a personal connection to that location. Once here, they're tethered to this place. The farther they go from it, the less they are able to retain their pre-death appearance," Lou explains.

What rips my heart out isn't the way they look—it's the way they sound. They're humming a soft melody with a haunting refrain. It wraps itself around my chest and squeezes out every drop of joy I've ever known.

"What is that? What are they singing?" I plead. "They have to stop."

"The longer they stay here, the worse it gets. A spirit is meant to move on, not linger. The humming is their souls crying. They're always crying, just at different volumes."

I find myself laughing. That laughter echoes throughout the kitchen and then takes over the house. It's an empty sound.

"So... what's the point? Huh? We get killed because of our skin and we don't even get a peaceful afterlife? *Are you kidding me?*"

I'm not sure when the laughter turned to sobbing, but

it has. Grandma holds me close and tucks my head under her chin.

"I didn't want to take you here, but I had to. I *had* to. It was the only way to make you understand," she pleads as she sways back and forth.

I pull away from her. "Why? What was the point of bringing me here?" I demand.

"There are souls that leave Jump houses and go on to the light. On to peace," Lou says, wiping the tears running down my face.

"How? How does that happen?" I ask.

"The fastest way is when the child's death is avenged. It doesn't need to be an eye for an eye. Let's say a kid is killed at the hands of someone for no other reason than the fact that they look like us. If that case goes to trial and a guilty verdict is found, that soul gets to Jump—go into the light," she explains.

"How often does that happen?" I ask. Both Lou and Grandma Sadie look away, telling me all I need to know. "This makes no sense. I would have heard about this many kids being killed," I conclude.

"Not all of them make the news. Everyone isn't always around with a cell phone handy. Especially the kids who were born in the era before cell phones. We have kids who have been around since the late eighties," Lou says.

That's when I recall the girls on the steps. And Donald. I now realize they aren't even from my time—that's why they're dressed like that. If what Lou says is true, they've been dead for over forty years.

"Lou is referring to the quiet deaths no one but the victims' close friends and family know about," Grandma says. "The deaths that take place in the back roads, late at night. The gunshot victim that the ER doctor makes little effort to save, because what's one less Black kid? There's more than one way your skin can get you killed, Lala."

I pull up the chair I was sitting on and slump down into it. I run my hands through my locs and feel the grains of sand embedded into my scalp. Why are there more of them now?

Lou takes a seat next to me, and Grandma joins us. Lou puts her hand on my shoulder and lifts my chin up so that our eyes meet.

"I come from a long line of custodians, women who are tasked with running Jump houses. And I have seen some heartbreaking things. I had to take in a little girl who didn't even realize her life was over. She still doesn't understand that she's dead, and certainly doesn't get why. But I have also seen some miraculous things like I witnessed back in April of 2021, a day of light, and it was spectacular!"

She exchanges a look of awe and gratitude with my

grandma. Whatever this "day of light" is, it makes them both happy. No, not happy... blissful.

"What's a 'day of light'?" I ask.

Lou replies, "That's the day a mass of souls gets to move on all at once. That day in April, I watched as the kids were suddenly bathed in brilliant light and then moved on to peace. You have not lived until you have seen something like that!"

"How does that happen? What makes it happen?" I ask.

I realize the answer even before I've finished asking the question. The last time hundreds of souls Jumped all at once was when the George Floyd verdict came in—April 20, 2021.

After viewing the brutal video of George Floyd's murder, a rash of marches began. They grew into a nationwide reckoning, unlike anything we had seen in over a decade. The protesters' rage and frustration with those in power was palpable.

George Floyd's death was a stark reminder that everyone who looks like me is alive but by the sheer "grace" of the system. And that system can change its mind at any given moment.

I feel yet another chill ripple through me.

"Why didn't all the souls go during the marches?" I ask.

"We don't choose who goes," Lou replies. "And some of the souls go after the events of 2021. There is no order."

Grandma puts both hands on my shoulders and looks deep into my eyes. "This isn't just about making life better for our people now—it's also a chance to get the ones who came before into the light. There are souls who have been here for decades. They deserve to find peace..."

Grandma falls silent.

My heart cracks open as I say out loud what Grandma was hesitant to say: "And to get peace, they need a movement..."

TWENTY

GRANDMA AND I BARELY TALK ON THE FLIGHT. When we land, we get in a cab and I drift off into space, pulled into a black hole where light cannot penetrate. I don't pay attention to what's around us or where we're headed. So when the cab pulls into a fancy circular driveway, I'm taken aback.

"What are we doing at Rue's house?" I ask.

"I know how hard this has been on you. I thought spending the night with your best friend might help. You will have to get up early so you can come home and change your clothes before school."

"What about Dad—is he okay with it?"

"While you were with Lafayette, your aunt called. She told me your dad could use some time alone."

I nod. "I saw a Flash of him breaking up with Candace. I guess it happened today."

"Makes sense. When I called to check in, I suggested you stay at Ruby's tonight. He leaped at the chance to be alone."

"What about everyone else in the house?" I ask.

"Your aunt and I are taking Arlo out to dinner. That'll give your dad some space for a few hours."

I want to be happy that I get to spend the night with Rue, but it's nearly impossible to feel anything in this void.

Grandma is suddenly fidgety and can't maintain eye contact. She goes to say something, but no words come out.

"Grandma, what is it?" I ask.

She signals for the cab driver to wait and tells me to get out of the car. Once we're alone, she exhales and comes out with it. "I'm sorry, La. I don't mean to keep pushing this, but I need to know with one hundred percent certainty that you understand the situation and that you will not interfere with the gold Flash."

I study her and note the intensity in her eyes. "Flashing really is the only thing that matters to you," I mutter.

She asks me to explain.

"I overheard Dad saying all you cared about was Flashing. I guess it's true."

"No, of course that's not all I care about."

"So, he was wrong—you didn't hold it against my mom when she lost her gift?"

"'Lost' is not an accurate description of what happened. Your mother took her gift for granted. She messed with it, and in the end, she paid the price," she says in a stern voice.

"Oh my God, you're still upset with her? She's been gone five years, and you still can't let it go?"

"It's not that simple, La!" Grandma tenses her jaw, and her body stiffens. I can almost feel the rage coursing through her.

"If this is how mad you are five years later, how angry were you back then? What happened between you two?"

Grandma shrugs. "It was a long time ago. I can't remember everything that happened between your mom and me." She presses her lips together to form a tight line, letting me know she is done talking about it.

"Grandma, please. I need to know."

She clears her throat and says, "Mercy was seven when she got her first Flash. It was the night before the first day at a new school. In the Flash, she saw herself in the lunchroom, laughing among a group of new friends. And because of that she was able to sleep well, knowing that her first day of school would be a good one. And it was.

"That night she told me how much she loved knowing something others didn't. She said it was like time was telling her a secret. It made her feel special. But it was more than that. I think the unknown made Mercy anxious. And the Flashes took that anxiety away. It also made her feel both special and powerful. So she wanted to expand her vision. She wanted the universe to reveal all its secrets to her."

Grandma falls silent. I don't think she's run out of words; it's more like she doesn't like what she has to say next. "After she nearly died drinking that vile concoction that was supposed to expand her gift, we realized her visions were gone completely. Flashing is a gift but it's also a responsibility. I was deeply disappointed in her. Although I tried my best to hide it."

"Mom saw through it. She knew how you really felt," I reply.

Grandma's eyes fill with tears. "I just...didn't know how to forgive her."

I bite my lower lip to keep from losing it. I can't think. I just need to be somewhere else right now. She calls out and says goodbye. I'm all out of words, so I just tip my chin toward her. She gets in the car and looks back at me as it pulls away.

Before I go inside, I call my dad. If I don't check in personally, he'll break down the door to Rue's house. I ask how he is, and he says he's fine. He asks how the day was with Grandma, and I, too, say it was fine. The conversation is short, since we're both lying to each other.

It's only when I'm at Rue's front door, hugging her, that I realize how much I needed to see her. She takes one look at my face and asks what's wrong. And before I can answer, she says, "Let's go to my room."

Ruby lives in a lavish modern mansion, with large columns, marble flooring, a grand staircase, and gorgeous bay windows. All the countertops are made of Italian marble, her kitchen is state-of-the-art in every way, and I swear a family of forty could fit into any one of her five bathrooms.

The first time I came over to her house and saw how she treated the staff, though, I knew she was my kind of girl. She asks how their day was, she cleans up after herself, and she never forgets any of their birthdays.

When we enter the house, the first person to greet us is Kimmy, the head housekeeper. She's also Ruby's favorite. Kimmy's always there for Ruby when her grandmother, Nana Dee, tries to make her feel bad about how dark her skin is. Kimmy has the same complexion. She gets what it's like to be teased, because the same thing happened to her when she was growing up.

"You girls need anything to eat?" she asks.

"Maybe later, thanks, Kimmy!" Rue says as we charge up the steps two at a time, desperate to avoid running into Nana Dee, who is visiting again. We get to the second-floor landing; we're only three yards away from our destination. Suddenly, we hear someone clearing her throat softly behind us. Rue and I silently bemoan our bad luck and turn to face her.

"Hi, Nana," Ruby says, barely able to keep the dismay from her voice.

Nana Dee is tall, lean, and has the posture of a seasoned ballerina. She's wearing a chic white button-down shirt with a black ball-gown skirt. Her jewelry is expensive yet understated. She has a perm, allowing her lustrous gray hair to be obedient. It's styled in a conservative, yet sophisticated updo.

Oh, and she smells good. She *always* smells good. I asked about it once, and Ruby told me her perfume was created just for her by the people at Chanel.

The thing that I love and hate about Rue's grandmother is that she gives the best shade of any Black woman I've ever met. When she insults you, it's so subtle, you think maybe you're imagining it. And normally I would be somewhat amused by it, but right now, I'd love to put her on mute. I'm not in the mood for her elitist, color-struck crap.

She greets Ruby, but all the while she's looking over at me. She's scanning my clothes to see if she approves. She doesn't. I'm wearing jeans and a sweatshirt.

"Good afternoon, Laveau," she says.

I have told her a million times that she can call me Lala, but she never does. She thinks my nickname is silly, and that since my parents named me Laveau, that is the name I need to be addressed by. That is to say, Nana Dee likes to stand on formality.

This is around the time she usually starts in on my hair. She hates locs and thinks of them as a symbol of chaos and a gateway to criminal behavior.

"I see you've opted to continue wearing your hair... like *that*," she says in a polite, placid tone.

Here we go...

"I still like locs, so... yeah. I'm still wearing my hair like this," I reply, resigned to dancing this same dance every time we see each other. "Don't you like it?" I ask, mostly joking, since I know the answer already.

"I think your chosen hairstyle is consistent with everything I know about you," she replies.

See? Shade.

"And how is your family, dear? Your father, your brother,

and, oh, that ever-so-animated aunt of yours? Are they all well?"

Nana Dee and Aunt J detest each other. They met a few times following a series of concerts where Rue and I performed. Aunt J thinks Nana Dee is what's wrong with the Black race. And Nana Dee thinks people like Aunt J gave birth to the "loud, angry Black woman" stereotype.

"Everyone's fine, thanks!" I reply, refusing to let her get to me.

"Good. I understand that you're spending the night with us?" she says.

"Yup. If that's okay," I add.

"Well, it is a school night. And even if that were not the case, it is customary to give notice before showing up at someone's home. Be that as it may, this is my daughter's home, not mine. And she allows for a loose interpretation of proper etiquette," she replies.

It's all I can do not to groan and roll my eyes.

"Ruby, the family photographer is coming next week. Perhaps you can start thinking about what you'll wear, sooner rather than later?" she says.

Ruby nods curtly. "I will."

"And Ruby, be mindful of the colors you choose. It's hard enough finding a photographer to put you in the right light. Let's not make it even harder for him."

Ruby says, "No problem!" While she says it with a smile, it's hard to miss the daggers coming from her eyes.

Nana Dee studies her grandchild as if seeing her for the first time. She reaches out, places her hand under Ruby's chin, and tilts her head back so they can make eye contact. "You really are very pretty," Nana Dee says. Ruby and I both know that what she means is that she's pretty *for a dark-skinned girl.*

Thankfully, Nana Dee says goodbye, and we find shelter behind the closed door of Ruby's bedroom. She decorated the room so that it's just as sparkly as her personality. The color palette is silver and rose gold. She has a crystal chandelier, a white fur rug, and a silver-tufted headboard with crystal studs. The bedding is plush and layered in high-end sheets and designer throws.

I go over to her bed and sit down. She comes and sits alongside me.

"Sorry about Nana Dee. I bought 'witch be-gone,' but it was expired," Ruby jokes. "With everything going on in Davey, my parents didn't want me to stay here with just the staff while they are out of town."

"Did something else happen?"

"More and more members of Faith and Honor have flooded into town. The opening of the Manor is only two days away, and everyone knows that's why they're here: to start some drama."

"Just another day in good old Davey," I reply with disdain. "Anyway, don't worry. Nana Dee is the least awful thing that's happened today."

"I'm ready for an update—whenever you are," she says.

The thought of having to recall all of today's events is just too overwhelming. I didn't plan to cry, but I didn't know how to hold it all in. Ruby leans over and says, "Shh, don't cry, it's okay. You don't have to tell me anything until you're ready. There's a math assignment that I'm trying to avoid, so take your time," she teases.

It's another half hour before I stop blubbering long enough to talk. I tell her everything, including the conversation I had with Grandma in the driveway. She doesn't interrupt. When I'm done, she looks stunned.

"Holy sh—" She stops herself. Her family are not big fans of swearing. And although she tries to rebel against it, that habit of not swearing has stayed with her. I know she has a ton of questions about ghosts, going back in time, all of it. But to her credit, she holds back and instead says, "I'm so sorry. This seems so unfair, La. You have to deal with all that pressure from your grandmother."

"Rue, fair or not, I've already made my decision. I just don't know how to live with it," I confess.

Ruby places her hand on my back gently. Her cell dings, and she looks at the screen.

"Who is that?" I ask.

"Mark—his parents were supposed to come back this evening, but their flight was delayed until tomorrow night," she says. Mark Winters lives only two blocks from Ruby. His parents are hippies; they champion just about every cause there is. They can be a little out there, but still really nice.

"What does he want?"

"He asked me to come and hang with some of his friends. Don't worry. I won't go. We can just stay here."

Mark is hopelessly in love with her. He has been since first grade. He goes to a different school now, but that doesn't stop him from inviting her to every party he throws. When she asks if I want to come, I usually say no. But there is nothing usual about today.

"We should go!" I reply, standing up, newly energized at the thought of getting away from how I feel.

"Are you sure?" she says.

"Yes. I need a distraction. Can you think of a better one than a party?"

Sneaking out of the house on the north side to go to a party after sunset probably isn't a good idea. I can admit that.

But it's only two blocks, and I would give anything to get out of my head right now.

We wait for Nana Dee to go to bed, and then we head for the back door.

On the way to Mark's house, we go by a number of Confederate flags that his neighbors proudly display. I swear there are a lot more now than the last time I was on this block. But there are no large pickup trucks or motorcycles roaring by with Faith & Honor members. No one is calling us names or threatening us in any way. In fact, there is no one on the streets but us. But that doesn't do anything to take away the uneasiness I feel. I take Rue's hand and can't help but note how cold it is.

She lives around here and walks freely—except at night. Her parents don't let her out after dark, unless she is being driven. Sometimes Ruby sneaks away, but she hasn't done that lately—not since the protests against the Manor began.

Ruby and I quietly exhale; we made it to Mark's house. On his front lawn there's a bright sign that reads IN THIS HOUSE... and it goes on to quote all the things they believe in: BLACK LIVES MATTER, LOVE IS LOVE, and NO HUMAN IS ILLEGAL.

We knock on the door, and Mark greets us with his signature suggestive smile that he reserves only for Ruby.

"Hi, Ruby..." he says in what he thinks is a sexy, deep

voice. In reality, his voice is kind of high and whiny. But his red hair and freckles make him adorable. Ruby greets him, and he steps aside to let us in.

There are about fifteen kids here. The lights are low and the music is loud. Everyone is chatting, dancing, and having a good time. Mark takes Ruby aside and tries whatever new pickup line he's discovered on her. I can tell from where I'm standing that he has failed.

Ruby makes her way back to join me. We head to the table that has soda and junk food, but that's not what I'm looking for. I need to forget everything just for one night. And if what I see in the movies is true, there's only one way to do that.

I scour the table but there is no alcohol.

My prayers are answered when I see what I need across the room—an older girl making the rounds, offering to pour a clear liquid into people's cups. I'm guessing it's vodka.

I go over to the would-be bartender, and before I even get the word out, she grabs an empty cup on the table and fills it. I shout over the music and ask her what it is. She confirms it's vodka.

"La, are you sure this is a good idea? You don't drink. Ever," Rue says, taking the cup from me.

"Maybe if I drink a little, things won't hurt as much. Or even better, maybe I'll forget about everything."

She thinks about it for a moment and reluctantly hands the cup back to me.

I sniff. I sip just a little. This could very well be the worst-tasting thing on planet Earth. How can adults drink this mess? It doesn't matter. The desired effect I want right now is oblivion. I want my mind to go blank. So I gulp down the drink. It burns my throat and makes me wince.

She sees the face I make and tells me to grab a can of Coke from the snack table and mix it in. It tastes only slightly better.

I feel like I have ingested liquid fire, and I desperately want to stop. But the goal is to forget all the bad things. So I keep going.

"More, please," I say.

The girl adds more to my cup, and I take another sip.

"Lala, that's enough!" Rue says, reaching out to take the cup from my hand. I don't let her.

I gulp down the rest. I feel warm and tingly all over. My face is flushed and the room is turning into liquid. Everything is beginning to blur and shine, but in the most beautiful way. I'm light as a feather. The weight that was placed on me is gone.

"I gotta get to the next room—you want one last drop before I go?" the girl says.

I reply with a goofy grin, "Hell. Yeah."

"La, don't!" Ruby cautions.

I tune her out and place my cup underneath the bottle of vodka. The girl pours for me once again. This time, I just chug it all down. I throw the empty cup on the table and walk to the center of the dance floor.

The bass comes to life as the new Megan Thee Stallion song comes on. Everyone in the crowd is jumping up and down, losing their minds, me most of all. I am no longer responsible for anything or anyone.

Suddenly, it hits me—there's a way I can be free from all of this. I run to the bathroom and lock the door behind me. I search the drawers and find what I need. I stand in front of the mirror, feeling the little grains of sand embedding ever deeper into my hair.

I can't see them, but I know they are there, just under the surface. I'll make it so that they have nowhere to hide. A triumphant smile spreads across my face.

I turn on the clippers and delight as my locs rain all around me. No more hair; no more racism.

I am.

Finally.

Free.

TWENTY-ONE

I'M NOT SURE HOW IT'S POSSIBLE, BUT THERE'S A gorilla playing racquetball inside my skull. I've never had a headache this bad. It's so intense, even silence is too loud. All I know is that I'm lying down on something soft. I'd love to pop both eyes open and spring to my feet. But right now, even the thought of moving makes me tired.

Get up and find out where you are.

It takes a moment, but finally, I summon enough energy to open one eye. And immediately, I wish I hadn't. There's a ray of light streaming through the window, and when it hits my eye, it feels like daggers stabbing my cornea. I groan and close my eye again.

"Little girl, don't even try it! Up!" a familiar voice demands. It's Aunt J. Her words ring out in my head as if she has a megaphone right against my ear. *Go.*

I make myself open both eyes and use my hand to block the light. When everything comes into focus, I realize I'm lying on the small red sofa in the back office of Aunt J's hair salon. I'm wearing an oversize shirt with the salon's logo on it. I groan again, desperately wanting to go back to sleep.

"You heard me, up!" Aunt J barks.

"Shh" is all I can manage.

"You must have lost *all* your good sense, telling me to shush. Laveau Janice Russell, get up, right now!"

It's rare for Aunt J to take a hard stance with Arlo or me. She's usually chill and, as a general rule, more fun than most adults. But right now, her no-nonsense tone is hard to miss. I'm pretty certain if I don't sit up on my own, she'll drag me up.

My head is not only throbbing, but it weighs the same as a Mack Truck. It takes everything I have, but I sit up. I was so focused on my headache that I'm just now noticing other things that are wrong with me. One, my mouth is super dry. I don't remember being this thirsty in my life. Two, my whole body aches. Lastly, my stomach will revolt if I even so much as look at food.

Aunt J is sitting across from me on a folding chair. She's watching me with a mix of disapproval and disappointment. There's a great combo to wake up to. I open my mouth and croak out, "Water, please."

"Humph." She goes over to the mini fridge in the corner then returns with a bottle of water and sits back down. She rummages around in her handbag, which is hanging off the back of her chair. She hands me two small white pills.

"What are these?" I ask, reaching for the water.

"Oh, so now you care what goes into your body," she says, rolling her eyes. "These are aspirin. They will help you deal with one of the many gifts left behind from drinking alcohol—your bad headache."

I take the pills from her and down them with the whole bottle of water. The temptation to lie back down is very strong. But so is the pissed-off expression on Aunt J's face. And I'm guessing that giving in to my desire to go back to sleep would only make things worse. So instead of lying down, I prop my elbows on my thighs and let my head collapse into my hands.

"How did I get here? Where are my clothes?" I ask in a gravelly voice.

"Ruby called, early this morning, and told me that my niece is stumbling drunk at a party she's not supposed to be at. Not only did you drink, but both you and Ruby got the bright idea to go out at night on the north side, like you're new here!"

"It was only two blocks," I reply.

"I don't care! You don't go out after dark over there. Hell, you can barely do that in this part of town."

"I know, I'm sorry. Why did you bring me to the shop?"

"I didn't want to risk your dad seeing you like that. I brought you here to clean up and get yourself together. I washed your clothes—they're in the dryer. They should be ready by now. La, I didn't think you were capable of doing something so stupid."

I scoff miserably, "You'd be surprised what I'm capable of. I know I am."

"What does that mean?" she snaps.

"Nothing," I mumble.

I need to ask her a very important question, and to do that, I'll have to make eye contact with Aunt J. So I chance lifting my head to meet her gaze.

"Are you going to tell my dad?"

"Oh no. That's your job. He needs to hear it from you. Lucky for you, he was called into work early. So you have until after school to think of a way to explain your actions."

"Don't you have to pick up Arlo and drop him off to school?"

"No, I switched with Grandma Sadie. She's gonna take Arlo, and I'll take you. That way we can have a nice long chat about just how much trouble you're in."

I start to feel bile in the back of my throat. The water that was such a blessing to me is now threatening to come back up. I run to the bathroom down the hall and throw up, twice. And now my stomach is completely empty. I drag myself to the sink and clean up.

I look at my reflection in the mirror. My face is ashy, my eyes are red, and although Aunt J was kind enough to put a bonnet on my head, I'm pretty sure my hair is a mess. I don't even dare look at it.

I sit back down on the sofa and wonder how long before the aspirin kicks in, because my head is still killing me. Why do they make drinking look so harmless on TV? Argh! It was such a bad idea—what was I thinking? How did being drunk help me at all?

"Now, where were we? Oh yeah, all the dumb decisions you made last night..."

Aunt J goes on to tell me that after I'd had more than my fill of alcohol, I became loud, belligerent, and unruly. I danced on furniture and threw up in Mark's coat closet.

But the worst thing I did came after all that.

"Did I get into a fight with someone?" I ask.

"No. You started talking nonsense. You yelled out to

everyone about how you were gonna fix this town and make everything better."

And suddenly, last night comes back to me in a rush: the drinking, the dancing, and, oh yes, shaving my hair off.

Oh. My. God.

I put my hand on my head. I look at Aunt J, silently pleading with her to tell me that I didn't do what I think I did. My first instincts are to take the bonnet off and see my hair for myself, but I'm scared.

"Might as well face it," Aunt J says, as if reading my mind.

She walks over to her shelf stacked with hair supplies on the opposite end of the office. She comes back with a large handheld mirror. She gives it to me. I reach up and slowly pull the bonnet off my head.

Yup, all my locs are gone.

I wait for the flood of tears and regret to flow through me, but it doesn't come. I should be shocked and horrified at what I did, but I'm not. This is nothing compared to all I saw yesterday. And what I will have to watch taking place tomorrow. So what if my head is shaved?

"I know how important your locs were to you. Are you okay?" she asks, worried.

I shrug. "Yeah, it's whatever."

Aunt J's jaw drops. She takes my face in her hand and firmly turns me toward her. She studies my eyes as if she expects to see a deep, dark secret revealed inside.

"La, are you on something?"

I laugh wryly. "No, Aunt J, I'm not on drugs. Promise. I just don't feel like making a big deal out it."

"I still have the hair you cut off. I can stitch it back on, no problem."

I shrug again and remind her it's just hair.

Without warning, we're surrounded by the sound of breaking glass. Aunt J and I exchange looks of panic and run to the front of the store. Someone has thrown a brick through the shop window.

Outside, there's a convoy of large pickup trucks and motorcycles, all proudly displaying larger-than-life Confederate flags as well as flags with the logo of Faith & Honor. The drivers are all wearing American flag face coverings so we can't identify them.

They stay in their cars or on their bikes, revving their engines and cursing at the store owners, who come out to see who's vandalizing their businesses. They begin to chant, "One, two, three, keep the north side n*****-free!" They chant it over and over again.

I'm standing right in front of the window, and I can feel Aunt J tugging on my arm to pull me to the back room.

My eyes are fixed on one of the men; he's wearing a dark red jacket. All I can see are his eyes. The man is over six feet tall, with stark blond hair and icy blue eyes. He catches my attention because he's not shouting in anger or acting wild like the rest of his crew. Instead, he looks calm and composed as he laps up the chaos they have brought to us. The level of hate I see in his eyes stuns me. It's as if we know each other and I have wronged him in some deep, unimaginable way.

I'm so focused on the look in his eyes that I don't pay attention to the person next to him. And I should have, because that guy hurls yet another brick through my aunt's window.

"Lala, down!" Aunt J shouts, pulling on me. The brick is just shy of hitting me. If Aunt J hadn't pulled me to the floor...

She orders me to crawl with her to the back room. The sounds of horns honking, more glass breaking, and men chanting make up the soundtrack as we move toward the back. My aunt gets her hands on her cell and calls the cops.

It's five minutes later when we hear police sirens off in the distance, and so does the gang. They take off down the road.

My heart is racing, and I am shaking from nearly

getting hit with a brick. I can't think. Aunt J looks me over three times to make sure I'm okay. I tell her I am, but she needs to make sure for herself.

The cops spread out and talk to the shop owners one by one. When they get to Aunt J, she says she didn't see anyone well enough to give a description. I can tell by the tremble in her voice that she's still in shock.

The shop owners are upset and outraged as they gather and talk among themselves. Mr. Harris, who owns the BBQ place down the street from the shop, grunts. "If them PCP people would let things alone... We don't need to go over to the north side. Don't nobody want to start nothing. Now all of our businesses are in danger. What sense that make?"

Mrs. Gordon, who owns the hair supply shop across the street, agrees. "Like we don't got enough to deal with! That PCP organization is gonna ruin what already took forever to build," she says bitterly.

The man who runs the dry cleaner next to the salon stands in stark opposition. "Them PCP people have the right idea. Why the hell can't we live where we want?" Mr. Monte adds.

"Will is right. Enough is enough. I'm glad the building is opening tomorrow. Who the hell are they to keep us out?" the old lady from the deli says as she takes in the damage done by the brick thrown through her shop's window. She spits out a litany of curses that would impress most sailors.

With everyone talking at once, the cops are having a hard time getting them to answer questions. I would have thought the loudest voice in the group would be Aunt J. She's always one to stand her ground and let you know what she feels and why. She reminds me of a lion: strong, loud, and protective.

But she doesn't do that. Instead, she makes us go back inside.

She says, "I'm gonna call Nicole to have her come look after the shop until I get back. You need to get going before school starts."

"School? Seriously? Aunt J, do you know what just happened?" I demand loudly, despite my still throbbing head.

"Yes, I was there. Now go get your clothes out the dryer. Or we'll be late."

ARGH!

How can she just act like it's nothing? That's so not like her. How is she not livid? *I'm* so pissed off, I'm grinding my teeth, hard enough that my headache is back. I feel my whole body tingle with rage, and my hands won't stop shaking. I try to focus on the task at hand.

I fetch my clothes and put them on.

My mind takes me back to the man with the red jacket. He loved watching his friends terrorize us. It gave him some kind of twisted pleasure. I recall those cold, dead eyes. He wasn't just comfortable in the chaos; he *thrived* in it. In order for the man in the red jacket to be okay, he needed to know that he could scare us. It's just like the troopers on the bridge on Bloody Sunday. Cowards.

We can't just give in to that. We can't have some random hate group trying to rattle us. That's bull, and I know Aunt J feels the same way. So what's her problem?

I march back into the front of the shop to tell Aunt J the truth. I don't care about school or anything else. All I care about right now is getting them back for what they did to us just now.

When I get to the front, I see a sight that stops me cold—Aunt J is off in the corner, doing something I haven't seen her do since Mom's funeral. She's crying.

The lion is exhausted.

TWENTY-TWO

WHEN I GET TO SCHOOL, FAITH & HONOR AND what they did is all over social media. And now there's thread after thread of people trying to identify the members behind the face coverings. But for every one person attempting to denounce the gang, there are three who applaud what they did.

I'm walking toward my locker, trying in vain to stop thinking about the airborne brick that came straight at me. I'm lucky Aunt J pulled me away. But then I wonder how many people weren't so lucky.

"Lala! Hello? Can you hear me?"

I look up and see Ruby heading toward me, waving her hand in my face. "Oh, I didn't see you," I admit.

"I've been calling out your name for three minutes! I thought you were ignoring me. I'm sorry I called your aunt, but I wasn't really sure what to do."

I shrug and assure her that I'm not mad. She tells me she almost had a heart attack when I shaved my hair off. But she thinks Aunt J did a good job wrangling my hair into an even, sculpted low fade.

"It looks so cute and trendy," she says. "What do you think of it?"

"I like it, too," I mutter. The truth is, I couldn't care less about what my hair looks like; it does nothing to stop the feeling of all the sand embedded in my hair.

"So what happened when Aunt J took you home?" she asks. I update her on everything.

My cell beeps, reminding me that I have missed calls from Dad, Arlo, and Grandma. They all left messages, but I can't deal with them right now. I put my cell away. Rue objects.

"You have to at least text them, La. You know your dad—he'll come down here if he thinks you're in danger. So just text and ease their minds."

I do as she asks. I text everyone that I'm fine, and then head for class.

I see Wes, Alex, and Ford talking among one another in the halls. They are looking at their phones. I'm guessing they're watching a video of what happened earlier. I just stand there for a moment and take them all in. What would I say to them?

I sigh and make myself turn away. The school day drags on. I pay no attention to the lessons in any of my classes. My teachers scold me for being so distracted.

What happened this morning becomes the talk of the school and makes its way into our classrooms. The principal makes an announcement, just before lunch, about safety and asks us to walk in pairs, as if that will help. After lunch I drag myself to another music class. My teacher asks me a question, but I miss it, too lost in thought.

"Ms. Russell, I know it's been an eventful day, but I still need you to focus on the lesson at hand," Mr. Rowdy says.

"An eventful day?" I repeat, disgusted. I get up and walk toward the door.

"Where are you going, Ms. Russell?"

I reply, "To the bathroom. Maybe by the time I come back, you'll find a better word to describe a group of hateful bastards terrorizing innocent people. You know, something better than 'eventful.'"

He calls after me, but I don't stop. I march down the hall, and with every step, I feel my blood boiling even more.

I don't go back to class.

In fact, for the first time ever, I skip not one, but two classes. I hide out under the bleachers. And when the final bell rings, I run to the bathroom and wash my face. I've been crying, but it's not like all those other times. These are tears of anger.

I latch on to either side of the sink and hang my head. I don't know what to do with this much rage.

"Hey, sis, you good?" Zora asks as she comes out of one of the stalls.

I nod. She walks over to the sink next to me and washes her hands. "The new style is fire. It's bold and unexpected. I didn't know you had it in you," she admits.

"Yeah, I'm full of surprises," I reply sardonically.

"Ruby told me about your aunt's shop. I'm sorry."

I don't say anything back. I just give her a slight nod, then look away and bite my lower lip to keep from imploding.

"You don't seem good at all. Your vibes are seriously dark right now," she says.

I scoff, "Yeah, that's the problem—my vibes."

"Is that the first time you've been that close to members of a hate group?"

"Yeah," I reply, looking at her curiously.

"That explains it."

"What, you've had close encounters with them?"

She nods. "Different group. Same hate. Back when we used to live in Alabama."

"What happened?"

"My dad worked at a factory there and had gotten a promotion. Some of the guys who worked on the team wouldn't take orders from him. It got to be a huge deal, and he needed to be escorted to his car at night. It got out of control, and finally Dad said we were moving. We had to go somewhere safe."

"Safe?" I laugh bitterly. "And you picked Davey?"

She laughs, too. "I was eight then. We have relatives here, so Dad wouldn't have to pay for childcare."

"I'm surprised you're not joining the counterprotesters at the Manor. I thought you'd be front and center."

"We did join—before things got violent. Now, none of our parents wants us to go. I get it. Still, I wish I could be there," Zora says. She studies me. "Something's changed in you, sis. Something more than your hair. I can feel it from here."

"Let's just say it's been an enlightening few days," I reply.

"Come to the meeting," she offers.

"Why, Zora?" I say, leaning against the wall. "Please tell me—what is the point of Black Alliance, of any of it?"

"It's really the only way to help you."

"How? *How* can you help me?" I snap.

"That fire that's burning its way into your chest, that frustration that makes you want to scream and break things..."

"Let me guess—if I go to Black Alliance, I won't feel that way anymore."

She replies thoughtfully, "No, you'll still feel it. But you won't be alone in it."

I tell Zora to go ahead and I'll join her in a minute. I text my dad and tell him to pick me up an hour later than usual. He's not crazy about my staying after school; luckily, I convince him that I am, once again, fine.

When I walk in, Alex gives me a charming, crooked smile, which makes my stomach do a somersault. I wave at him and take a seat. The group of about twenty kids is seated in a circle, listening to Wes, who is in the middle of a story.

"Last year, my little brother went to the children's museum in Houston on a school trip. I went along as a chaperone. I saw these two kids from a different school: a cute little white girl and an adorable Black boy. They had to be about five or six years old. They must have gotten separated from their group, because they were wandering around the front of the museum, looking lost.

"They saw a cop car driving by. She had this look on her face—relief and joy. She got excited and yelled, 'It's Mr. Police Officer! Let's ask him!' So she went to wave at them. The Black boy wagged his finger in her face and said, 'Ay, no cops.'"

Everyone starts laughing. Wes chuckles along and then waits until the laughter dies down before going on. "The little girl turned to him and said, 'Police help people.' You could see it was at that exact moment that the boy realized he and that little white girl had led very different lives."

The Black kids in the group continue to laugh, not for the humor of it, but because it's a moment they can all relate to.

"Their teacher found them, and they got on their bus. On our ride home, I was cracking up! I couldn't get over the certainty in that little boy's tone. I mean, what could you be into, at five years old, to be afraid of the cops?"

Up until that moment, Wes is enjoying telling the story. But after the laughter dies down, his face falls.

He continues in a quiet tone, "It wasn't until later that I realized I don't remember ever *not* being afraid of cops." The room falls silent. Wes has traveled somewhere else in his mind, leaving us in the room without him.

"That look of relief that little white girl had—that little boy will never experience it," Zora adds.

"Sometimes it's just one of these things you gotta get used to," Ford says. "Like when you all see me, I'm me. I'm a handsome, sexy, charming, brilliant musician. You know, I'm Ford, baby!"

Everyone groans, and Ford pops his collar like he's in a hip-hop video.

He continues, "But when I go down certain streets, enter certain stores, I can see the way some white folks look at me. They reshape me into a delinquent, a savage, a dangerous monster. But I don't care. I look them dead in the eye."

Alex replies, "Yeah, well, that's your first mistake. 'Cause you keep looking at some white folks, and the way they see you, won't be long until it's the way you see yourself. I'm not about to take that chance. I just keep my eyes looking straight ahead."

"Yeah, but why should we have to avoid eye contact just because we encounter certain people who look down on us?" Rue asks. "Nah, we need to look them in the eye. I'm not doing that 'head down, eyes on the floor' thing. Sorry. That's just a little too Jim Crow for me."

"So is avoiding eye contact an act of self-preservation or cowardice?" Zora asks.

The whole group starts talking at once. They don't all agree on one point of view, but everyone argues their thoughts passionately. I stay silent and focus on the three boys. They're so alive with opinions and emotions. The spark within each of them is undeniable.

I pit the boys' fervent hunger for true equality against the hatred spewing from the guys in the pickup trucks with giant Confederate flags. The guys in the trucks can wrap themselves in a snuggly, warm blanket of ignorance.

Wes, Ford, and Alex, on the other hand, can't afford ignorance, because not knowing comes with consequences. So they, like the rest of us, have to know which streets they can go down and which ones to avoid. They have to learn the right posture, tone of voice, and mannerisms needed so that they aren't perceived as a threat.

I don't realize the pen I picked up from the table is digging into my hand until it breaks through the skin. I put it down and wipe the drop of blood on my dark jeans. That's when I notice my hands are shaking.

I guess that's a sign of even more anger, but this time, the anger is directed at me. I spent all this time sleeping on just how dangerous it was to look like me. I knew it in my head, I saw the articles and TikTok videos, but I didn't let any of it sink in.

I preferred to let music take me away to a deep, all-consuming state of slumber. The three boys, Rue, and Zora—they didn't do that. They've stayed awake, despite the mind-numbing exhaustion that comes with being awake.

"Look at it this way—we can't even get the principal to grant us a meeting about getting the Confederate flag down from the front of the school," someone says. "Even after we got over a hundred signatures."

"Maybe we should start smaller and see if we can get the flags in the display cases removed first," Rue replies.

I stand up as if a bolt of lightning has struck me. "What flags?" I ask.

That's when they explain that all three of the display cases throughout the school, showcasing awards and certificates, have a backdrop of a pinned-up Confederate flag.

"You didn't notice that?" someone asks. I don't know who said it, because I'm too busy searching my mind—and oh yes, I remember now.

I saw the flags inside the displays the first day of school, my freshman year. And yet, as the days wore on, I erased them from my mind. I walked by them hundreds of times and blocked them out. The flag on the pole in front of the school is impossible to ignore. It waves hello to us every day school is in session. But all the other flags, the ones that sit in the displays, in a place of honor and reverence, I pushed to the back of my mind.

"How could you miss that?" Zora asks.

"I missed a lot of things," I reply. My hands ball into fists and my chest heaves up and down rapidly. My nails dig into my palm, and I like it. I like the pain because it tells me I'm not asleep.

I grab the music stand near the door and flip it upside down so that it becomes a makeshift weapon. I yank the door open and march out to the hallway.

I scream at the first display, *"ARGHHHHHH!"* I lift the stand just above my shoulders and smash it into the glass.

"Lala, what are you doing?" Rue shouts.

Everyone in Black Alliance has followed me out to the hallway and are begging me to stop. I don't take in what they are saying. The only thing I'm focused on is the glorious sound of glass breaking.

I yank the flag out of the display. It takes some effort to rip it in two, but not as much as I thought it would.

The boys in the club try to hold me back as I make my way down the hall and smash the second display. I wrench free of their hold. They're stronger than me—on any other day but today. The intense fury that's traveling up and down my spine causes my hand to shake as I make my way to the third display. That's when I feel a set of strong hands grab me and slam my face into the wall.

The security guard screams, "What the hell do you think you're doing?"

I let out a dry laugh. "Waking up..."

TWENTY-THREE

THE SCHOOL CALLS MY DAD. HE COMES AND HAS a meeting with the principal that lasts about half an hour. I have to wait outside, so I have no idea what they're talking about in there. I could almost see the smoke coming out of Dad's ears when he arrived. In fact, his head looked like it was going to explode and take me with it.

He comes out of the principal's office and, without breaking stride, says, "Let's go."

I get in the car, not sure what fresh hell awaits me. I've never been in this much trouble before, and were this any other day, I would be terrified. But while I care that Dad is angry with me, there is no love lost for the display or the racist flag it held in high esteem. I don't regret what I did, at all.

Dad hasn't said a word on the drive so far. I can't stand the thought of disappointing him. I know I messed up, but I'm not sure just how much. Will they kick me out of school? Dad worked so hard to be able to afford the tuition, and if I get thrown out now, it'll really crush him. I trained for hundreds of hours over the years to get into the school.

I would never have said this a week ago, but if I'm expelled, I think I'll eventually get over it. Dad, on the other hand, I'm not so sure.

"Are you going to say anything?" I dare ask, unable to stand the silence any longer.

"First, your grandmother has the nerve to take you on some out-of-state field trip, without asking me. When I demand an explanation, all she says is 'It had to be done.' And now you go and do this?!" he growls angrily, gripping the steering wheel.

I've never had to ask this question before, but it feels like I should: "Dad, do you hate me?"

He takes a deep breath but doesn't say anything. We drive in silence for what feels like forever. And then, just when I think Dad won't reply, he starts talking.

"Nothing could make me hate you or Arlo. Not one thing."

His statement should be comforting, but it isn't. There's something matter-of-fact in his tone. It's just an inescapable fact that he loves me, but that doesn't mean he *likes* me at the moment.

"Since I'm already in trouble, I guess I should come clean about the other stuff," I suggest.

I told Aunt J that I would let Dad hear about my drinking from me. I have no doubt in my mind that if I don't confess, she will tell him. If it had been something minor, she'd let me get away with it. But something like drinking pushed the limits too far.

So I tell Dad about going to a party down the block from Ruby's and how I drank myself sick.

"I know. Your aunt told me."

That makes sense. When Dad first walked into the school and saw me, he wasn't shocked by what I'd done to my hair. I guess Aunt J really did tell him everything.

"She said she'd let me tell you," I reply.

"I pushed because I knew she was hiding something. I always know when she's hiding something."

I inhale deeply and try to embrace the wrath that's coming my way. Dad goes back into silent mode.

"Dad, say something."

"Like what?"

"Like how disappointed you are that I drank. How

stupid it was. And how foolish it was to walk on the north side after dark, even if it was only two blocks."

He takes a quick look at me and then puts his eyes back on the road.

"What about school? Have I been kicked out?" I ask.

"We'll talk about what you did today when we get home. I need to speak to both you and your brother. And now, as far as the drinking goes..."

"I'm grounded. I know. For how long?"

"Six months."

"*What?* Dad, that's—"

He shoots me a look that makes the words shrivel and die in my throat. I grit my teeth but don't respond.

"You're getting two months for each infraction. You drank. You went out after nightfall. And you lied about where you would be spending your evening."

"I didn't know that I was gonna go to the party—it was a spur-of-the-moment thing," I reply.

"So it's okay to make bad decisions when they aren't premeditated?"

"That's not what I'm saying. I just...I didn't set out to go to Mark's house."

"And that's another thing—I have never met Mark. I don't know his family and what they may or may not be into. Drinking underage is unacceptable. But drinking around people you don't know is even worse. Something bad could have happened to you, something more than just vomiting your guts out."

"Ruby was with me."

"It doesn't matter. Both of you were reckless. I talked to Ruby's parents, and she's grounded, too. At least she had the good sense not to drink. So she's only grounded for a few weeks, from what her parents told me."

"It wasn't her fault. I made her go. She didn't want to."

"Doesn't matter. If you'd let Ruby talk you into sneaking out, I'd still punish you. You are responsible for your choices, Laveau. You know that."

I hang my head and pray for this day to be over. But then I remember what it would mean if today really were over.

Dear God, someone is going to die tomorrow. And I won't do anything about it.

I think back to everything that happened in New Orleans: the museum, the jubilation and hope I felt visiting 1965, and, of course, the soul-crushing visit to the Jump house. And because of all those things, I now fully understand why the Flash has to take place. I will not change my mind about that. But it does raise the question: What kind of person am I?

Dad sighs. "Okay, you don't need to go into deep

sulking mode. I might reduce your time to five months, but it will depend on how you behave."

I turn toward the window and look out at the streets and houses as they blur by. "No, Dad. Six months is about right. I'll do the time."

He groans. "La, stop being so dramatic. It's not like I'm sending you to jail."

No, but maybe that's where I belong...

When I get home, everyone knows what happened at school. Arlo and my aunt have questions that I can't answer. What was I thinking? How did I expect to get away with such a blatant act of vandalism? What led to shattering the display? Dad puts a stop to the questions and asks Arlo to get started on dinner.

Grandma takes me aside and says, "Is this my fault? Am I the reason you started acting like this?"

"No, it's not you," I promise her.

"I knew taking you to the Jump house could backfire," she says. I've never heard her sound so guilty and so full of self-doubt before.

"Grandma, you didn't send me the gold Flash. This isn't your fault."

She frowns and shakes her head. "Okay."

Arlo calls us in for dinner. He decided that since Aunt J and I have had horrible days, he would make one of our favorites for dinner: chicken and dumplings. Arlo places the dinner plates in front of us. Aunt J is so busy checking social media, she hardly notices.

"These Faith and Honor idiots have been posting warnings all day about what'll happen if the Manor opens tomorrow. They really think they can stop us?!" she says.

"Aunt J, you've lived in this town forever, why does this stuff still surprise you?" I ask.

"You're right, La. Sometimes I really hate this place," she answers, shaking her head in frustration.

I scoff, "Only sometimes?"

"Not everyone is counting the days until they leave Davey, La," Arlo says.

"Well, I am. I'm counting the days, the hours, and minutes. It's been 'fun' being on a steady diet of small-town racism. However, I'd like to try something else."

"Janice, you had a long day. Put the phone down and eat with us," Dad says.

She looks up from her phone. "Huh?" We all look back at her. She sighs and puts her cell down. "I just want to be kept informed," she says.

"Don't worry, Aunt J, there'll still be chaos after dinner," Arlo assures her.

"Did you hear back from the insurance company?" Grandma asks.

"Not yet. I'll call them again tomorrow," Aunt J replies.

Dad clears his throat. "I wanted to make it official—it looks like Candace and I are done," he says awkwardly.

We all look at one another, not sure of the right thing to say.

"I'm sorry, Earl," Aunt J replies. "I know you really cared about her."

"Thanks," he says.

"But I could have told you that it wouldn't work. That's what happens when you stray too far from women with 4C hair."

Dad laughs, which takes us by surprise, no one more so than Dad himself. "Next time I fall for a woman, I'll be sure to have you come by and inspect her curl pattern."

"Deal," Aunt J replies.

"So, is no one gonna ask Lala why she cut all her hair off?" Arlo says. "Because the suspense is killing me."

I suck it up and tell them about the night at Mark's house. I'm not sure what's more of a shock to Arlo: my new haircut or my getting drunk. Well, either way, it's safe to say he's stunned. His mouth is open and has been for a good twenty seconds.

"Close your mouth or say something," I tell him.

He folds his arms over his chest and replies, "I'm not really sure where to put my emotions. On one hand, I love this 'act out to make up for never acting out.' But as your twin, it worries me that I'll soon be an only child. Because if you keep going like this, Dad will kill you. And once again, I'm torn. I mean, if you're not here, I could turn your room into a game room. But then you'd be dead. So, again, not sure where to put my emotions."

I decide to ignore my brother and instead see how much trouble I'm in. I turn to Dad as Grandma and Aunt J look on.

"Am I getting kicked out of school?" I ask.

"No. But your principal talked about filing a police report. Thankfully, I talked him out of it. It helped that you have never been in trouble before this," Dad says.

"Thank goodness! But I'm sure they didn't just let it go," Aunt J says.

"No. Lala, you're suspended for the rest of the week. And you're on probation. If you don't cause any more trouble, they'll take the suspension off your record. I told them to send me the bill for the glass display."

"I'm guessing you'll take the money for the display out of my allowance?" I ask.

"No. I'm not punishing you for breaking the display," Dad says.

We all look at him as if he's lost it.

"Wait, you're not gonna punish Lala? We are allowed to wreck school property and not get in trouble? Why wasn't I told of this? My life would have been so different had I known that," Arlo quips.

"Arlo, hush!" Grandma says.

"You two clean up the dishes and meet me in the family room when you're done," Dad says to me and Arlo, getting up from the table.

Later, we join Dad in the family room like he requested. We've rarely gone there since Mom died. It was her favorite room, and I think the memories are still too fresh. There are photos of her everywhere, making this both my favorite and least favorite room in the house.

All three of us sit at the card table where we used to play spades. That was a long time ago—we don't play anymore, for the same reason we don't come into this room often.

"I know that things have been even more difficult than they normally are in this town. When your aunt told me about the brick, it felt like someone had poured cement into my chest. I could hardly breathe. I feel the same way when Arlo leaves the house. The thought of losing you kids is too much to even think about."

"We're here, and we're okay," Arlo assures him.

"He's right—you're not gonna lose us," I add.

He smiles sadly and nods. "When I was growing up, I didn't have to work hard to find a reason to hate and fear white people. I was always seething with rage because of one racial incident after another, after another. I sealed in my hatred for white people. And I was not gonna change my mind."

"You're not like that now, so what happened?" Arlo says.

"What happened was your mom passed out right after delivering you two. The nurse on duty was a white woman named Denise Martin. She went into action quickly and basically saved her life. And even when the doctors came and took over, Denise was never too far away. She came in to check on your mom even on her day off. She had this sincere desire to see your mom get better. I couldn't make that fit with what I thought all white people were like. It confused me."

Dad looks over at a framed picture of Mom on her birthday. She's grinning as she blows out her candles. And we are standing alongside her.

"I talked about it with your mom, and she told me what I'm about to tell you: There is no such thing as 'good white people' or 'bad white people.' There are people. Some of them are led by fear, like the hate groups we see around here and on the news. But don't go thinking that hate groups are the majority. They are not the largest group; they are just the loudest."

"Yes, they're loud," I mutter to myself, recalling all the shouting and cursing the Faith & Honor members were doing at the shop.

Dad puts his hand on my knee and says, "La, I didn't ground you for breaking the display, didn't even ask you why you broke it, because I *know*. I know what it's like to have to choke down your rage. I know it seeps out of your pores and makes you do things you'd otherwise never do."

I think back to the display and how much fury was running through me. I wanted to keep going and going until it was all just a tower of broken glass.

"You and Arlo need to find a way to deal with what you're feeling—breaking things or hurting people is not the way to go. I don't want to lose you kids to this town. I also will not allow you to be driven by rage and anger. That's just another way to lose you."

The man in the red jacket with the icy stare comes back to me. "They hated me, Dad. I looked in one guy's eyes, and he just wanted me to stop existing."

I catch Dad wince as the thought hits him. "I know, La. It must have been terrifying to be so close to that much hate. But that's why it's important you don't let hate stay with you. It'll spread. And so there will not be any difference between you and them. You get angry, then play video games, get on the treadmill, play Grace. Do whatever you can to get it out safely. And be done with it. Do you two hear me? We don't hate in this house. And we don't let rage drive us. Am I clear?"

We both mutter, "Yes."

"Good, because while you got away without punishment this time, next time you won't be so lucky," Dad warns. "I mean it. You can't control the hate people send your way, but you can control what you do about it. And you will."

"I had to smash them, Dad. It was like those flags were mocking me. Mocking us. I had to do something. All this time, I've been running away from this kind of drama. But I don't want to do that anymore. I want to protest and scream and chain myself to stuff," I admit.

Arlo looks at me like I've lost it, but I don't care. It's how I feel.

"I thought I could go far away, but New York City is just Davey with skyscrapers," I say. "I want to be in the front, lead the charge. It took so much just to get this far, and now, it's not far enough. I want to push us further along."

"And breaking the display was a good place to start?" Arlo asks.

"No, that's not what I'm saying," I snap.

"You're saying you want to be part of some kind of revolution? Fight the racism and stand your ground, is that it?" Dad asks.

"Well, yes! I do."

He smiles. "There are ignorant people who think that all Black kids do well is get arrested and play basketball. You're a classically trained cellist, attending a top-notch conservatory." He places both hands on the sides of my face and looks deep into my eyes. "Lala, sweetheart, you *are* the revolution."

TWENTY-FOUR

I WAS UNDER NO ILLUSIONS. I KNEW I'D NEVER BE able to sleep. So instead, I talked to Ruby for over an hour. We talked about everything but what was really on our minds. She filled me in on school gossip, celebrity gossip, and even gossip from her neighbors. And then she started in on reality shows and YouTube influencers. She knew those things didn't matter to me, but she also knew I was desperate for a distraction. When I heard her yawn, I told her she could go to bed. And before signing off, I told her how much I loved her.

"I love you, too. Try to sleep," she said just before hanging up.

After speaking to Ruby, I caught up on homework. Cleaned my room and read five chapters of the book we were assigned in English. I can't say that I retained much of it. I just needed to do something to keep my mind occupied.

Once I see the sun coming up, I go down to the basement to play Grace. I think she's missed me, maybe just as much as I've missed her. I don't practice the pieces that we are working on in class. Instead, I play the pieces that I have known how to play for years. It's comforting to play what I know.

I leave the basement and find Aunt J in the kitchen, getting breakfast ready. As always, soul music is playing in the background. When she sees me, she furrows her brow.

"La, you look so tired. Did you sleep last night?" she asks.

"Yeah, a little. I'll take a nap later," I promise her.

My dad enters the room. "She's right, La. You look like you could use more than a nap. Since you don't have school, come have some breakfast, and then you can go back to bed. And after you've rested, I wrote out a list of chores that need to be done around the house. Since you're home, might as well be useful."

"All right, I'll clean the house," I reply.

Dad crosses his arms over his chest. "Oh really, just like

that? You're not going to point out whose turn it is to do what?"

I smile. "I'm here anyway. Like you said, might as well."

The truth is that manual labor could very well keep me from losing it.

Arlo comes down from his room and rushes to the table, saying he's starving. Aunt J made a feast, but I just nibble on the end of my dry toast. I can't eat anything. The three small bites I take fall like rocks to the pit of my stomach.

My family goes about their daily morning routine, but I feel out of step with them.

Aunt J updates us on the opening. She announces that there are more than enough counterprotesters to rival the hate groups that are there with their signs. She tells us she's going to join them as soon as breakfast is over. I can tell, from his low growl, that Dad is not a big fan of that plan.

Grandma Sadie enters looking haggard. I'm thinking she and I had the same kind of night. She pours herself a cup of coffee, never once taking her eyes off me. She's trying to gauge how I'm feeling. I don't know what the expression on my face tells her. The fact is, I've been through just about every emotion there is. And now, I'm just...here.

"You kids make sure to say a proper goodbye to your grandmother. She's going back home—later today, right?" Dad says. There is no denying his threatening tone.

Grandma smiles but it doesn't quite reach her eyes. "Tomorrow evening."

"You'll be missed," Dad lies. Grandma nods and gives Dad yet another fake smile.

In less than an hour, the house clears out, leaving only Grandma and me. We clean up the breakfast dishes, vacuum the living room, and do three loads of laundry, all without saying a word. I guess she feels like me—she needs to be busy, no matter what.

It takes two hours, but the house is spotless, and all the chores on Dad's list have been taken care of.

I go to my room in the hope I'll find something to do so that I am not locked in with my thoughts. I look at the time on my Apple Watch, and it's still hours away from 7:07.

Grandma knocks on my door and peeks in. "I was just checking to see how you are."

I'm not sure words have been invented yet that could convey how I feel, so I just shrug. She comes to sit on the bed beside me.

"I've been thinking about where we should be when it

happens. I would love to go to church and maybe light a candle for the family. Would you like to come with me? I think it will do you some good."

"I can't. I have to be there when it happens."

"What? No, Lala!"

"Don't worry. I know I can't stop the Flash. I get why this has to go down the way it will. But there is absolutely no way I'm leaving this kid alone. The least I can do is be there. I want the last thing he sees to be a sympathetic face, not that cold bastard and his shotgun."

"No, absolutely not! Believe me, I understand wanting to be there, but it's not safe. Who knows? Maybe this old man takes another shot, and his next target is you. Lala, I love you for the size of your heart and all the compassion that you fill it with. But going to that old man's house is unacceptable. I'm not changing my mind. You are to be nowhere near there."

"That's unacceptable! I have to go."

She jumps to her feet. *"I said no!"*

Grandma doesn't usually yell. She's always been composed, never needing to up the volume of her voice. But the woman I see standing before me is rattled, wide-eyed, and overwrought. She's almost to the point of hysteria.

My mouth drops open. I'm not sure what to say. I think

Grandma's reaction has surprised her, too. She takes a moment to collect herself.

"I don't know how I can make any of this better for you. But I certainly won't allow it to get worse. You will not go anywhere near that house. Am I making myself clear, child?"

I nod.

"I need to hear you say it."

So I stand up and reassure her, out loud, that I will not go to the old man's house.

"Good. I'm gonna go downstairs and start lunch," she says.

"I'm not hungry."

"Neither am I," she admits. "Nevertheless, lunch is coming right up."

In the past week since my birthday, I've been on a never-ending ride of emotions. If they gave out medals for existential crises and uncertainty, I'd take first place. And yet right now, on this issue, I am one thousand percent certain that being there is the right thing. I don't give a care what could or might happen to me—this kid will not die alone.

I see all three boys in my mind's eye, followed by a wave of nausea. I can't help but wonder what they had for breakfast. Did they casually wave goodbye to their families, believing they'd see them again? If they knew today was their last day, what would they rather be doing than going to school?

I'm thinking some adventure somewhere, or maybe playing for a packed concert hall. But something tells me that all three would rather be spending their last moments with family. I think that's what I would want for myself.

For one crazy moment, I consider telling all three of them what I saw. I know it's ridiculous, because first of all, they won't believe me. And second, telling them could change the Flash in a hundred different ways. And if that happens, it would affect the movement that's supposed to come about following the shooting. Oh and let's not forget, changing something could result in unforeseen consequences to my family.

I lie down under my covers and close my eyes, knowing full well that sleep, like peace, will elude me.

It's just six in the evening when we all gather at the kitchen table. I don't know what Arlo made or what I put in my mouth. I'm a ghost of myself and have no real connection to what is happening around me. Aunt J shows us her feed, an endless stream of videos and pictures of Black protesters in action, refusing to let the hate group stall or stop the opening.

The procession of Confederate flag trucks and bikes is back and has added to its numbers. Some people have been there all day, from early morning until now, just as night is falling. The only thing I can think about is the fact that today, someone's world will end.

Grandma has barely touched her food and is in deep reflection mode.

I have to leave the house in the next half hour to make sure I'm there in time to see the Flash play out. I think I can climb out my window, but I've never tried before, so I'm not sure if it'll work.

We're just at the tail end of dinner when Aunt J shouts, *"OHMYGOD!"*

We all turn to face her, not sure what's got her so upset. She's looking at her cell and her chest is heaving up and down. We watch as a flood of tears makes its way down her face.

"Janice, what's wrong?" Dad says, getting up from his chair to make his way over to her.

She answers in a weak, watery voice, "It's on fire. The Manor is on fire..."

We all take out our phones and get on social media. Meanwhile, Dad goes over to the TV in the living room and turns it on to the local news. According to the news and multiple witnesses on social media, someone on a motorcycle from Faith & Honor hurled a Molotov cocktail through a window and fled.

The building is in flames, and the horde of people who were inside are running for the exits. We watch, stunned, as additional cops, EMTs, and firefighters arrive on the scene. The firefighters work quickly to try to get everyone out. The cops bring out their riot gear as an already out-of-control crowd becomes a mob.

Aunt J is calling around, trying to get the status of her friends who were down there. The panic on the screen is mirrored in the living room. Grandma closes her eyes to pray, and I'm pretty sure that Dad has been holding his breath since he turned on the TV.

I can't let the mayhem shock me into standing still. I need to make moves. While my family is fixated on the news, I quietly run to my room. I search the back of my closet and pull out an old pair of kicks Dad got me the year before last. They're red, shabby, and the fit is a little snug. Oh well, they'll have to do since I left my other sneakers in the basement. My heart is pounding, my skin tingles, and my fingers are cold and unsteady. I open my window; there's a cold wind in the night air, the kind of wind that chills you to the bone.

I grab my new Black Alliance jacket from my closet, zip it up all the way, and crawl out the window. When I'm two blocks away, I call for an Uber. The old man doesn't live too far from the north side. I look at my watch—it's 6:35. I have just over half an hour to get there.

That's when it hits me—I won't know what to say once I find myself looking down on a boy's lifeless body. I want to say something that's meaningful and will leave him at peace. Grandma would know what to say. I should have looked up a prayer or something. Or even a poem, anything. But it's too late now—the Uber pulls up to the old man's house.

I can't believe I'm actually living inside the moment I saw a week ago. The same moment I've been dreading. The house looks just like it did in my Flash. I look over at the white door, no more than a few yards away. This is it. This is where it happens.

I crouch beside a Jeep that's parked in front of the house. I have a good view of the house, but anyone coming down the street won't be able to see me. I look at my watch; it's 6:50. I look over to the right and see someone coming my way.

Wes.

TWENTY-FIVE

DAMN IT!

Wes is dressed exactly like the boy in my Flash: black jacket with Black Alliance logo, Apple Watch, and red sneakers.

I didn't *decide* to pop out from behind the Jeep; my body just kind of did it on its own. I needed to see Wes. He's looking around, concerned.

"Hi, Wes."

He jumps back. "Oh, damn! Where'd you come from?"

"I was hanging out with a friend who lives near here. And now I'm just waiting for my Uber."

"Oh," he says, looking up and down the block, uneasy.

"Is everything okay?" I ask.

"Yeah, I'm sorry, La. I can't talk now. I have to find my brother." Wes is about to go up the steps to the old man's door.

"Wait, how did you lose Paul?"

"He takes art lessons around here. And with the stuff going on at the Manor, cops have been out and heavy. Sirens make Paul anxious; he's very sensitive to loud noises. He ran off. I'm going door to door to see if anyone has seen him. When he takes off, he doesn't go far. I'm sure I'll find him."

"Do you know if everyone that was inside the building is okay?" I ask.

"Yeah, I heard no one was seriously hurt. But the fire is still not under control. Oh, and breaking that display case, I totally get it. I hope you didn't get in too much trouble."

"Well, it's more like good trouble," I reply.

"Okay, I gotta go. Later."

He turns to go up the steps once again, and I latch on to his arm and gently pull him back toward me. "Hey, Wes?"

He looks back at me with growing suspicion. "Yeah?"

"I—You—" All the words I can think to say die in my throat.

"La, what is it?"

"You are a very good big brother. Paul is lucky to have you."

He grins. "Actually, my mom and I are the lucky ones. He's really kind of awesome. Except when he's beating me at chess. That hurts the ego a little."

I laugh. He does, too.

In that moment, looking at his concerned eyes and warm smile, I know.

"Wes, you shouldn't go up there and knock on the door."

He looks genuinely perplexed. All of a sudden, I hear the words that Dr. Davis said to me at the African American Museum.

"Never in all of human history has a movement taken place without the help of ordinary people..."

I hear Grandma's voice as clear as if she were here with me.

"This isn't just about making life better for our people now—it's also a chance to get the ones who came before into the light..."

The last voice that comes to me brings with it a comfort and peace that settles over me.

It's my dad's voice. He knew all along what I tried so hard to deny.

"Lala, sweetheart, you are the revolution..."

"La, hello? What is it? Why shouldn't I knock on that door?" Wes asks.

"Because I saw Paul, and he went the other way."

"You saw him?"

"Yeah, I didn't realize it was him. But thinking back, I'm sure now. He went that way," I reply, pointing away from the old man's house.

"Okay, thanks, La! I'll text you when I find him."

Wes runs in the opposite direction and then turns the corner, out of my sight.

I look at my watch: 7:00 p.m.

I wait at the bottom of the steps. I have several texts from Grandma Sadie and Ruby. There's also a handful of missed calls from them. I can't reply, I need to stay focused. My cell buzzes—I have yet another text, but this one is from Wes. *Found him! Thanks!*

It's 7:05.

I walk up the steps to the old man's house.

My movements are graceful and free of anxiety.

I now realize *I* wore the black jacket with the logo on the back that Zora gave me. I don't think I meant to wear it. Or did I? I don't know. Doesn't matter now.

It's 7:07.

I knock. Three times.

The door swings open.

The old man's eyes meet mine.

And right away, I know who he is.

I've never met him outside of my premonition, but I *know* him. We've encountered those vile and vicious eyes throughout history.

They've belonged to different people:

Savage slavers.

Lethal lawmen.

Poisonous politicians.

But although the faces change, the eyes are still the same. What's most disturbing about the windows to the old man's soul are the things that aren't there:

Care.

Compassion.

Courage.

My mind goes back to the story Wes told at the Black Alliance meeting about the little white girl and the little Black boy who got lost.

As I stand two feet from the old man's shotgun, I'm learning what the boy already knew: For the rest of her life, that little white girl would be the recipient of a priceless gift. It's one she doesn't even know to be grateful for—the gift of pausing.

Pause: to make sure it's really a gun and not a cell phone.

Pause: to make sure it's the right apartment number on the "no knock" warrant.

Pause: to make sure it's the right person being chased, not someone of slightly similar features.

No, for the rest of his life, that little boy knew he'd never receive such a present. And in this moment, neither will I.

The old man fires, just as a new gold Flash begins to materialize.

The shotgun muzzle sparks like firecrackers in the night sky.

The gold Flash and the sparks from the shotgun collide in the middle.

The force of the buckshot shreds through flesh and through bone; it sends me flying backward into the air. It brings with it the kind of agony the mind simply can't understand. I fall flat on my back. I've been disassembled, my insides on the cold concrete porch. A red river forms, made entirely of me.

I don't want the old man's face to be the last thing I see.

I don't want to die here alone.

That's when I smell it—jasmine. I look above me, and there she is, looking down at me. I am not alone. Arlo was right; her smile does radiate. Standing next to my mom is a small-framed Black woman with a kind smile and a determined gaze.

Abigail.

She doesn't need to tell me who she is. My soul knows her. She comes armed with a multitude of resilient and formidable souls; they gather around me. Most are new faces, but some I recall from the exhibit at the museum. They are activists, going as far back as Abigail's time, 1795. They are all standing over me, triumphant and proud.

That's when I realize that my ability to see the future really is a gift and not the curse I originally thought it was. A small smile forms on my lips. And just before the last sign of life drains from my body and the darkness takes hold, Abigail whispers, "Not yet, child. Open your eyes and look!"

I use all my strength to keep the nothingness at bay, long enough to follow her gaze. And there, in the ocean of blood, a series of gold Flashes plays out. I'm watching multiple parts of the future, each showing a different glorious moment that is to come.

There are a hundred or so people of different backgrounds, holding up signs that read NOT ONE MORE CHILD. *The crowd is passionate and steadfast as they march through the streets of Davey.*

A ripple appears on the surface of the bloody river, changing the image in the Flash: The marches grow to several thousand. The people wear shirts that proudly display what part of the country they are from and where they stand: NEW ORLEANS SAYS, "NOT ONE MORE CHILD." According to shirts, there are protests taking place in New York, Chicago, Los Angeles, Houston, and Philadelphia.

The ripple continues to flow and the images change again. This march is in Washington, DC, and has ballooned to hundreds of thousands. It's an army of families with T-shirts, posters, and banners of their children and the words SAY HER NAME.

The next Flash that appears in the blood is of the old man with the shotgun. He stands before a judge. There's no sound. But she slams her gavel, and the sheriff comes to take the old man away. The crowd in the courtroom leaps to their feet.

Farther down the crimson stream, a new Flash: It's the north side of Davey. There's a long line of people waiting to enter the grand opening of an African American museum. And across the street from the busy event is the Manor, newly remodeled. The residents consist largely of families of color.

A new gold Flash appears right after: families, glued to the TV as they wait with bated breath and watch the news. The well-dressed anchorwoman announces the passing of what has come to be known as "the Davey Bill," which prohibits Confederate flags on any and all public buildings. She announces that while it's not yet federal law, many states have put police reform measures on their ballots for the upcoming elections. And among the newest states to be added to this list is Texas.

The final gold Flash is of me, surrounded by all the kids at the Jump house. We're standing amid the luscious and fertile ground of the backyard. The place is set up for a concert. Everyone is dressed in all white. Auntie Lou places a gold chair in front of me and then hands me Grace.

But Grace has changed. She's now all white and has a glossy finish. I sit in the chair, take Grace in hand, and play. The melody is one I have never heard before. It's complex and beautiful. It's unexpected and yet oddly familiar. As I play, one by one, the kids change form to brilliant beams of light. They ascend one after the other. A calm peace looms over the yard.

I'm the last soul left. Auntie Lou says, "I lifted the veil. They needed to see you one last time."

Someone comes behind me and places their hand on my shoulder—it's my dad. Arlo, Aunt J, and Grandma stand next to him. They look content and serene. I play a refrain of the piece I played before. I am suddenly engulfed in light and am airborne. I look down on the Earth below; all that remains is Grace.

The feelings of newfound hope and resolve that washed over me when I traveled to 1965 return, even as I lie dying. I now know that in times of strife, struggle, and spilled blood, we are never alone. We stand with the ones who came before us.

Do not be afraid of the path we must walk, or be overwhelmed by it. We did not build this bridge. We had no say over its weak construction or its faulty design. The trek across is deliberately dangerous and willfully unsteady.

But we, who are no longer flesh, have looked ahead. And we can confirm that yes, we do make it to the other side.

MARIE ARNOLD was born in Port-au-Prince, Haiti, and came to America at the age of seven. She grew up in Brooklyn, New York, alongside her extended family and attended Columbia College Chicago with a focus on creative writing. Marie is a *New York Times* and *USA Today* bestselling indie author under the name Lola StVil. Over two million readers have downloaded her young adult fantasy series, Guardians. She is also the author of *I Rise*, *The Year I Flew Away*, and *I Was Told There Would Be Romance*.